I0731790

The Strange and Curious Cases of

Roscoe Brown

Detective, NYPD

A Novel
by
M. Ward Leon

© Copyright 2020 M. Ward Leon

No portion of this book may be reproduced in whole or in part, by any means whatsoever, except for passages excerpted for the purposes of review, without the prior written permission of the publisher.

For information, or to order additional copies, contact:

Beacon Publishing Group
P.O. Box 41573 Charleston, S.C. 29423
800.817.8480| beaconpublishinggroup.com

Publisher's catalog available by request.

ISBN-13: 978-1-949472-14-1

ISBN-10: 1-949472-14-1

Published in 2020. New York, NY 10001.

First Edition. Printed in the USA.

All rights reserved.

A pithy cop quote goes here.

Roscoe Brown Cases

The Case of the Mad Hatter

The Case of the Devil's Bite

The Case of 3 Wives Dead

The Case of the Dewy Decimal Demon

The Case of Never Odd Or Even

The Case of the Graves Creeper

The Case of the Glass Slipper

The Case of A Brush With Death

The Case of the HAD Matter

The Case of the Mad Hatter

"*Here is a bulletin from CBS News, in Dallas, Texas. Three shots were fired at President Kennedy's motorcade in downtown Dallas. The first reports say that President Kennedy has been seriously wounded by this shooting...*

"*...From Dallas, Texas, the flash apparently official President Kennedy died at 1 pm Central Standard Time.*"

At 2 pm Eastern Standard Time, Detective Sergeant Roscoe Brown was eating lunch at the Nathans Famous hotdog stand, on Riegelmann Boardwalk in Coney Island, the same lunch that he has eaten for over fifteen years, ever since he joined the NYPD. Two chilidogs, an order of crinkle cut French fries, and a cup of Joe, black.

The music on the radio was interrupted by the news of Kennedy's assassination. People stopped walking and stood still, people stopped eating and just sat staring at each other, everyone was in shock and disbelief. Time stood still, the air seemed to be sucked out of the room, people felt an enormous loss like they lost a close loved one, and of course they had.

Roscoe finished up lunch, put his coat and hat on, said goodbye to Vinnie, the counterman and headed back to the 60th precinct up on West 8th Street.

Waiting outside was his partner Detective Jim Walsh leaning against the building having a smoke. He straightened up when he spotted Roscoe coming around the corner, took a deep drag on his Lucky Strike and tossed the butt into the street.

"Hey Roscoe, did ya hear? JFK got whacked down in Dallas."

"Yeah, I heard. Just look around Jim, everybody's walking around like zombies."

"I can't believe it."

"Me either, I'm just sick to my stomach."

As they were going into the station, Patrol Officer Mike Lawlor was coming out to start his shift, "Hey did you guys hear, they just got the creep that shot the Kennedy!"

"No shit? Who is it?" Roscoe asked.

"Some Commie nut named Oswald, an ex-marine."

"You're kidding, an ex-marine!" Walsh said in disbelief.

"That's what they're saying. Hey, I got to go. I'll see you guys later. Oh, I almost forgot, Captain O'Rourke wants to see you two."

"Yeah, see ya Mike." Roscoe said as they entered the station.

The whole station was a buzz with dozens of news flashes: some true, some false and on top of that all kinds of crazy rumors were floating around. By the time Roscoe and Jim made their way upstairs to the Detective's squad room, the latest story was that this guy Oswald was the point man to some twelve Soviet hit men, most of them from an elite sniper unit stationed outside of Moscow who had parachuted in from Cuba last night and had positioned themselves in not only the book depository but several were on the roof of the downtown Howard Johnsons and hidden inside the giant ice cream cone atop the Dairy Queen.

Roscoe knocked on the Captain's door, then stuck his head in and said, "You wanted to see us, Captain?"

"Yeah, come on in fellas. Terrible thing, this whole Kennedy thing."

The two detectives walked in and sat down without responding, cause what can you say, except just a bunch of clichés that everyone's uses.

What a tragedy.

He was so young.

I can't believe it.

Who would have done such a thing?

What's this country coming to?

Poor Jackie.

I'm going to miss him.

He was cut down in the prime of his life.

Our thoughts are with the family.

Now what?

Roscoe and Walsh sat silently for a few minutes waiting for the Captain to say something, but he was deep in thought. Finally, Roscoe said, "Chief, you wanted to see us?"

"Yeah, right. Terrible thing, this whole Kennedy thing."

"What a tragedy. He was so young." Jim said looking down at his shoes.

"Terrible thing." The Captain sighed.

"Captain?" Roscoe asked trying to get him focused.

The Captain was actually crying for a moment, then snapped back to the present. "So, we got a homicide I want yous guys to investigate."

"Why us Captain, we're working three cases already." Roscoe asked.

"This was some big union muckety-muck, a real high profile case, so I want you and Walsh to get this one cleaned up pronto, capeesh?"

"Capeesh. Who is this guy?" Roscoe inquired.

"His name was Dickie Moffit."

"Dickie Moffit from the UHCMW?"

"The what?"

"The United Hatters, Cap, and Millinery Workers International Union. Gee Chief, everyone knows that."

The Captain looked at Roscoe in amazement, "Roscoe, you're just a wealth of useless information, you know?"

"Thanks Chief."

"That wasn't necessarily meant as a compliment."

"I know, so where can we find Moffit?"

"1186 Sheepshead Bay Road. He's upstairs sitting in his office with his brains splattered all over the walls. Go check it out and keep me posted."

"Okay Captain, we'll keep you in the loop."

As they were leaving the Captain's office, they heard him mumble, "Terrible, this whole Kennedy thing. He was so young."

!!☀️†☆⸪♣️💀❋⚡!!

By the time Brown and Walsh arrived at the scene, the M.E. was already there waiting for them. "Boy, you two sure took your time."

"Sorry, Doc it's this whole Kennedy thing, traffic's a mess." Brown said.

"You got a siren don't ya?"

"Take it easy Doc, what's got your shorts in a bind?"

"I'm going out of town for Thanksgiving."

"Oh, and you want to leave early?"

"Hell no, I'm going to the in-laws. I hate going there, it's such a hassle, the traffic's always a bitch and on top of that, did I mention it's with the in-laws?"

"Yeah, hate the in-laws, hate the traffic, hate the hassle, got it. So, whata we got here, Doc?"

"We got one Dickie Moffit, aka Dickie "the Derby" Moffit. He's been shot from behind at close range, I would say dead for at least six hours. No sign of a struggle, and from what the uniforms tell me there doesn't seem to be any forced entry, so maybe he knew the person who shot him. Any more than that, I'll know when I open him up."

"Thanks Doc. If we don't see you, have a happy Thanksgiving."

"Very funny, asshole."

And with that the good doctor took the body and left. Roscoe and Jim started the tedious task of going thru Dickie the Derby's life to see who decorated the walls with his brains.

"Jimmy, why don't you take the bottom floor and I'll take the upstairs. Tell the uni's no one comes in without our say so."

"Right, Roscoe."

Roscoe stood in the middle of the room and turned a slow 360 degrees. He stopped at every 90 degrees and just stare. Roscoe had a photographic memory of sorts, he could look at a crime scene and remember every detail of the area, no matter how minute. He could then reimagine the whole room or zoom in on the smallest section down to the size of a paperclip. After he memorized everything in and about the room, he started to go thru Dickie's desk.

Most of the items in the desk pertained to the business of the UHCMW, There were files relating to contracts with hat manufactures, names, and addresses of the union officers, names and addresses of all the union workers, and all kinds of financial reports.

Roscoe discovered Dickie's address book, and appointment calendar was hidden way in the back of the top right drawer behind a large cigar box filled with assorted hat bands. He didn't place much importance to the box of varied hat bands, he was more interested in the book of names and dates.

In the calendar, there were dozens of meetings over the last eighteen months with someone with the initials MJP, with the subject of someone or thing KGL. But in Dickie's address book, there wasn't anyone listed with the initials of either MJP or KGL.

On all the walls were photos of Moffit with world leaders from all around the globe. Pictures of him with Vice President Richard Nixon who was wearing a brown fedora, with Winston Churchill sporting a derby, Charles de Gaulle President of France with a beret, Lyndon Baines Johnson wearing a ten-gallon Stetson, Fidel Castro of Cuba wearing his green army cap, Prince Rainier of Monaco, J Edgar Hoover of the FBI, even Nikita Khrushchev of the Soviet Union just to name a few. There must have been over a hundred photos of Dickie with the world's elite, literally a who's-who of the crème de la crème.

Roscoe was duly impressed by the numerous connections that Moffit had with leaders from all over the world, Presidents, Prime Ministers, Ambassadors, Senators, Congressman, Kings, even the superstars of Hollywood and the sports world. But, as he was starting to leave the room he stopped and turned around, something didn't seem on the up and up. Maybe it was because of what happened today, but all of a sudden it hit Roscoe that there wasn't a photo of Dickie Moffit and John Fitzgerald Kennedy, the 35th President of these United States, now deceased.

"Hey, Jimmy. Come up here."

Roscoe waited for his partner seated on the sofa opposite the desk where the victim was found. He heard Walsh's size thirteen's clomping up the wooden stairs; he sounded like a herd of buffalo stampeding.

"Yeah, what?"

"So, I was noticing all the photos on the wall of Mr. Moffit with all these big leaguers."

"Yeah, so?"

"So, where's Dickie and JFK, I ask you?"

"What, you called me up here just because this jamoke's a freaking Republican. Who knows why, there could be a million reasons, maybe he doesn't like the Irish or maybe he was doing the horizontal greased-weasel tango with Jackie, who knows. What's that got to do with Mr. M getting a hole the size of a Zeppole in the back of his head?"

"I don't know, I just found it odd, that of all the heavyweights he got his picture taken with, that the one guy that's missing is Kennedy."

Jim said nothing, he just let Roscoe work it out in his head like he always did.

"Yeah, you're probably right. Did you find anything downstairs?"

"Naw, nothing really. His wife's at the station waiting for us."

"Okay, let's go talk to her.

On their way out of the house, an officer was standing outside by the front door, the cop was short, fat, disheveled smoking a cigarette.

"Hey, nobody goes in unless I say so." Roscoe told the uni.

"But, I'm supposed to get off in an hour."

Walsh got nose to nose with the sentry, so close his head touched the officer's cap and he snarled, "Listen to me you fat fuck, you'll stay here until somebody relieves you and if anybody enters this house your ass is grass. Understood?"

"Yes sir, understood."

Roscoe pulls the car up to the house as Jim finishes reprimanding the overweight constable. Jim gets into the passenger side looks at the officer at the top of the porch, slams the door as to put an extra punctuation on his dressing down.

"Nice touch, Jim."

"Thanks."

"Greased-weasel tango?"

Mrs. Moffit was waiting in interrogation room 1, the door was slightly ajar so she wouldn't feel she was trapped. Roscoe and Jim walked in each carrying a cup of coffee.

Roscoe asked, "Mrs. Moffit may I bring you something to drink? Coffee, hot tea or maybe a soda?"

"No thank you." She said with a small smile.

Delores Moffit, a demure woman in her late fifties, medium height, slightly overweight, not a beautiful woman, but she did the best with what God gave her. She was well dressed, she was wearing a basic black dress, very stylish, a single string of pearls, her hair was beautifully coiffed, and her makeup was exquisite. She wore a wide brim black wool felt hat with a matching ribbon. Of course, you'd expect the wife of the union president of United Hatters, Cap and Millinery Workers International Union to wear a hat, society expects nothing less.

"We're sorry for your loss, Mrs. Moffit." Roscoe said as he sat directly across from her, Jim set off to his partner's right.

"Thank you, you're very kind."

"Now Mrs. Moffit, is there anybody you can think of that might want to hurt your husband?"

"I don't know, he was the president of the UHCMW union and over the years he had bumped heads with a lot of people. But I can't think of anyone that would want to kill him."

"Well, what about someone in the union, someone who might have wanted him out of the way? You know, someone who might have wanted to take over."

"Richard never mentioned anyone."

"Richard?"

"Oh sorry, Dickie."

"Mrs. Moffit, can you tell me if you know anyone with the initials either MJP or KGL?"

"MJP. KGL. No, I'm afraid not."

"That's alright, I afraid I have to ask you where were you between the hours of 10 am and 4 pm today?"

"Yes of course, I was volunteering at the American Cancer Society."

"You were there the whole time?"

"Well, except for an hour when I went to lunch with my friend Tiffany Tomball. We ate at the Black Swan over on 14th Street. I can give you her number if you need it."

"Maybe later. Mrs. Moffit is there anyone you think we should talk to that might be able to help us in finding who killed your husband?"

"Well, Lou Addler was his best friend, if Dickie was to confide in someone, it would be Lou."

"And is Mr. Addler associated with the union?"

"No, he works for the government, the CIA."

Roscoe and Jim looked at each other with a surprised expression.

"The CIA? The Central Intelligence Agency?"

"That's right."

"Do you know how Mr. Addler and your husband knew each other?"

"Yes, he's our next door neighbor."

"Mrs. Moffit, we appreciate your coming down and speaking with us. Here is my card, please feel free to call me night or day if you think of anything, no matter how insignificant that you think it might be, call me. As they say the devils in the details."

"Thank you detectives, you've been most kind. Can I go back home?"

"I'm afraid not at the moment, we're still processing the crime scene. You understand."

"Yes, of course."

"Where will you stay?"

"I have a sister in Manhattan."

"Can we offer you a ride to your sister's?"

"Thank you no, she's on her way here to pick me up."

"Again, Mrs. Moffit we're so sorry for your loss and I want to assure you that we will do everything we can to catch your husbands murderer."

"Goodbye."

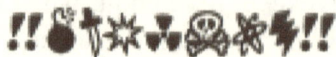

"Can I help you gentlemen?"

Roscoe and Jim flashed their badges to the receptionist and Jim said, "We're Detectives Brown and Walsh, NYPD Homicide. We'd like to see Agent Lou Addler."

"Do you have an appointment?"

"Yes we do."

"If you gentlemen would have a seat, I'll see if he's available."

The two detectives walked to the large red couch and took a seat. On the coffee table in front of them were dozens of general publications, Life, Post, Look Magazine and a copy of the New York Times newspaper. Roscoe picked up the Times and Jim grabbed the February copy of Life magazine with the picture of Alfred Hitchcock standing with a crow perched on his head.

Jim was halfway thru the article on Hitchcock's new thriller, the Birds when the receptionist hollered; "Mr. Addler can see you now."

Jim tossed the magazine down in disgust, "Figures!"

They were led thru what seemed to be a rat maze of corridors until they reached the office of Lou Addler, who was standing behind his rather plain wooden desk covered in files and papers.

"Please gentlemen, have a seat. You'll excuse the mess; they say a clean desk is a sign of a sick mind. How can I help you?"

"Thank you for taking the time to meet with us Agent Addler, I'm Detective Sergeant Roscoe Brown and this is my partner Detective Jim Walsh."

Roscoe held up a photo of Addler and Moffit, "Are you aware of the death of Mr. Moffit?"

"Yes, I heard earlier, I can't believe that anyone could do such a thing."

"We've spoken to his wife and she told us that you and Mr. Moffit were best of friends, is that correct?"

"Yes, I would consider Dickie to be one of my best friends. We've been next door neighbors for over fifteen years"

"Had he confided in you about any problems he might have had with any person, a company, or any government?"

"No, not really. Although, next month there is going to be union elections for officers and he did say there were a couple of guys who were running against him for President. And as you know union rivalries can get pretty ugly."

"Thanks, we'll check it out. Anybody, in particular, you think we should concentrate on?"

"Joey Rocco, a real goombah, if you know what I mean."

"Mafia?"

"Well, they don't call him "Joey Leathernuts" for nothing."

"You're kidding, right."

"If I'm lying, I'm dying."

"Leathernuts. Okay then, well here's my card if you think of anything else please call me. We appreciate your time Agent Addler."

"My pleasure, I hope that I may have been of some help and if there is anything I can do. And please, if you could keep me informed."

"Will do."

As the Detectives were leaving, Roscoe turned back to Addler and asked, "So, when did the CIA move to 2515 West Fifth Street?"

"September, that's why the place looks such a mess. Why?"

"Just curious. Thanks again."

Out on the street, Roscoe leaned into Walsh "So, Whatca think of our boy Addler?"

"I don't know there's something smarmy about this guy, I don't think he's straight up. You?"

"I agree, a bit of a weasel. I don't care if he's CIA, let's keep an eye on him."

"Got it."

"Let's go see this Joey Rocco, Joey Leathernuts and see what his story is. This guy sound like a real "gavone". Leathernuts, give me a fucking break. The dumber the nickname the dumber the goon."

!!💣†☆⚓.☠❋✦!!

Later that day, Roscoe and Jim were making their way to 7506 13th Avenue, Brooklyn, the home of the Wimpy Boys Club to meet with one Joey Rocco. For years it's been the home away from home for the head of the Colombo capo Greg Scarpa Sr. and his crew.

There, standing in front of the door and blocking the entrance of the club, stood two thugs both wearing black leather jackets, greased back hair, and black Ray Ban sunglasses, striking the traditional stoic arms crossed who the fuck are you pose. Roscoe walked up to the bruiser on the right, held up his badge and said, "Here to see Joey Rocco, he's expecting us. Now be a good boy and tell Joey Leathernuts that Detective Brown is here, capeesh?"

The big lummox looked at Roscoe with seething hatred, he slowly transferred the wooden toothpick from the right side of his mouth to the left. Waited for what he felt was long enough to show disrespect to the cops then said, "Yous wait here." before he went inside the club.

Joey came out five minutes later followed closely by the door gorilla right behind him. "I'm Joey Rocco, you must be Detective Brown. How can I help you Detective?"

"Is there somewhere we can talk, it's about the murder of Dickie Moffit."

"Hey, it wasn't me. I've been here all the time, right boys?"

Both hoods confirmed his being there.

"Yeah, but I didn't say when."

"Don't matter, I was here, right boys?"

"Right Joey, yous was here."

"Don't tell me, that one's studying to be a brain surgeon, right Joey?"

"Naw, he's more of a heart specialist. He can cut out a heart in seconds, right Vito?"

"Right Joey, yous was here."

"Let me put it another way, either we go somewhere or we go down to the station to talk?"

"Yeah the station, I'll meet you down at the 60th tomorrow at 11 am, and I'll be with my mouthpiece."

"Great, wouldn't want it any other way, see you then Joey Leathernuts."

"Listen, only my friends call me that!"

"Aw Joey, I thought we were friends, no? Maybe after tomorrow. Let's go Jim."

Back in the car, Jim made a point to drive passed the Wimpy Boys Club so Roscoe could wave at the gunsels.

"You know Jimmy, these hoods are the real deal bad boys. There's this story that's been floating around for years that one of the crew murdered a woman they feared would turn rat. The rumor goes that she was shot in the head, rolled up in a Persian rug and dumped. Four days later a dog was running around the club with the woman's ear in its mouth. They're not to be trifled with, they only respect brass balls, so never ever show fear."

Roscoe dropped Walsh off at his apartment and then drove back to Moffit's house; he felt he must have missed something. Standing in Moffit's office again, Roscoe had an uneasy feeling that he had overlooked something, so he started back from the beginning. He went thru every inch of the desk. As he was rifling a stack of papers in the bottom drawer, a key fell out on to the floor. The key was for a safe deposit box at the Mechanics & Traders Bank at the corner of Franklin Street and Greenpoint Avenue.

On his way out of the office he noticed something in two of the photographs of Mr. Moffit with a couple of the world leaders he was posing with, Fidel Castro and Nikita Khrushchev, and way in the background and slightly out of focus were two figures that looked eerily familiar, CIA Agent Lou Addler and Joey "Leathernuts" Rocco.

Roscoe couldn't be a hundred percent certain, but what and why would the three of them be seen with Fidel Castro and Nikita Khrushchev. He could kind of understand why Dickie "the Derby" would be hobnobbing with world leaders who all sported chapeaux, but what was a CIA agent, a Mafia mobster, and the head of the United Hatters, Cap and Millinery Workers International Union be doing together chumming around with these hardcore Commie leaders?

It was after 6 p.m., so the Mechanics & Traders Bank was closed, he would be there bright and early in the morning when the bank opened. He removed those two particular photos off the wall and took them with him after he scrutinized all the other pictures in Moffit's office and found there weren't any others with the dubious tripartite appearing in them.

On his way out, he made sure that all the doors were locked. He walked over to the squad car parked out front to make sure the two officers were not sleeping.

"You boys okay?"

"We're doing okay Detective."

"Great, no one goes in. This is a high profile case and if something goes wrong remember, shit rolls downhill. Good night, gentlemen."

Detective Sergeant Roscoe Brown, born and raised in Coney Island. Joined the NYPD right out of Queens College, City University of New York. Graduated top of his class, majored in Political Science, at one time thought of getting into politics, but after talking to a representative from the NYPD on career day, he signed up then and there. He was slightly overweight for his height, he still had a great head of hair, just starting to get a hint of grey on the side, he wore a Clark Gable mustache, always dressed in a suit and tie and was never seen without his trademark fedora. Roscoe always looked very tidy.

He's been a cop for twenty-one years, the last fifteen in homicide. Rated as one of the best in the city, partially because of his photographic memory, he's won dozens of citations and commendations for service above and beyond the call of duty and for heroism. He once saved a fellow officers life at his own peril and was wounded. He's won the respect of his peers and superiors and has been partnered with Jimmy Walsh for the last ten years. They were usually brought in for the strange and special cases, the hard ones and high profile ones.

Still single, but has a steady lady friend, Betty Armstrong. She has worked as a teller at Maspeth Savings Bank for nine years and is next in line to be head teller after old Mrs. Goldberg retires next year. Roscoe and Betty met eight years ago when Roscoe came in to open a checking account and she assisted him, he boldly asked her out to dinner and she said she accepted. Partially because her three brothers were all police officers in Massapequa, Long Island.

Roscoe and Betty hit it off immediately and recently have been seriously talking about tying the knot next June. Whenever his caseload allows they have dinner together, but because this one's tougher than normal he'd grab a couple dogs at Nathans.

Roscoe lives at 2831 West 19th Street between Neptune and Mermaid Avenues in a small brick attached house that he grew up in and took over once his folks moved to Miami Beach when his dad retired. And his girlfriend, Betty lives at 8121 20th Avenue and 82nd Street in a five-story apartment house in Bensonhurt, conveniently located just four blocks from the 20th Avenue subway for a twenty-minute ride to see Roscoe or vice versa.

Usually, he wouldn't have come over to see her, but the Kennedy assassination had really hit her hard. She worked on his campaign and had actually met him and Jackie at a rally and fundraiser. Betty was crushed, almost inconsolable by the time he arrived. She was sitting in front of the television crying when he entered the apartment, he sat down beside her and she turned and buried her face in his shoulder.

"Why? Why would anyone want to kill him?" Her voice was muffled being so close to him.

"I don't know, babe. I think it had to be more than just some lone crackpot."

"Do you really think it was more than just Oswald?"

"One guy couldn't have gotten off those many shots with such pinpoint accuracy."

"I just can't believe he's dead."

"Well at least they got Oswald, and they'll get to the bottom of this pretty quickly."

On the CBS News, they were showing pictures of Jackie dressed in her bloodstained pink Chanel suit standing next to Lyndon Johnson being sworn in as President on Air Force One. Mrs. Johnson pleaded for Jackie to change her clothes, but the widow was sending everyone a message to the world standing next to Johnson covered in blood. She told reporters, "I want them to see what they've done to Jack." She worn the dress for 24-hours.

Roscoe held Betty sobbing for three hours until she finally fell asleep in his arms. He laid her down on the sofa and covered her up with a blanket. Before he went to work, he left a note on the coffee table saying that he would check in on her in the morning and told her that he loved her.

‼️🩸🕇✳️🪰💀✳️⚡‼️

The Mechanics & Traders Bank wouldn't open until 9 am, and since he had the car, Roscoe stopped by Chock-full o'Nuts coffee café over on Avenue J to pick up a dozen donuts and a couple cups of the House Blend coffees, black.

Betty had just woken up and was staring at the TV, CBS was rehashing the story from yesterday, there weren't any new developments, too early. Everyone on the news looked like they hadn't slept, they were all unshaven and in wrinkled suits and shirts.

"Hey baby, how are you?"

"Still in shock, mmmm that smells good coffee and donuts, I love you."

"Thought you could use a little happiness."

"Mr. Morgan called, the bank's closed today, a national day of mourning. Maybe tomorrow too."

"Damn."

"What's wrong?"

"It's this case I'm working on, I need to look into this guy's safety deposit box that's at Mechanics & Traders Bank. This is really going to slow things down."

"So, do you have to go in?"

"Got to hon, I'm working on a high profile case, but it looks like it won't be a long day. I'll call you when I know what's what. And do me a favor don't just sit in here watching the television all day, promise me you'll go out and get some fresh air, promise."

"Promise."

Roscoe finished off his coffee and four glazed donuts, gave Betty a kiss and headed down to the station. Just to be sure he drove over to the Mechanics & Traders Ban and when he got there, there was a sign in the window proclaiming that the bank would indeed be closed until Monday, November 25th out of respect for President Kennedy.

Detective Brown walked into the squad room a little after nine, the buzz was still all Kennedy. As he walked thru the room back to his office he bumped into Captain O'Rourke, "How's the Moffit case going?"

"Still early but got a couple things I'm chasing down. I'll keep ya posted, seen Walsh?"

"Yeah, he's in your office."

Roscoe walked into his office to find Walsh reading the New York Daily News, the headline was "KENNEDY ASSASSINATED". The subhead, "Johnson was sworn in as President; Leftist Jailed as Slayer" the picture was Johnson and Ladybird trying to comfort Jackie.

"Hey Jimmy, what's the latest?"

"They say this guy Oswald was an ex-Marine, He defected to the Soviet Union in fifty-nine and came back to the U.S. married some Russian broad last year.

"After he shot Kennedy from the sixth floor of that book depository, he gunned down a cop on the street before trying to hide in a movie theater where he was finally arrested. He claims he was set up, that's he's just a patsy, the lousy creep. I hope they fry this guy. What do you think, Roscoe?"

"I find it hard to believe that he was a lone wolf, too much planning for one guy, and he doesn't look all that smart. Plus three marksman shots in less than nine seconds with a M91/38 bolt-action rifle at a moving target? Something smells fishy, we'll see."

"Anything more on our Moffit case?"

"Yeah, I went back to his place last night and while searching his desk again I found a safety deposit key for the Mechanics & Traders Bank, but they're closed until Monday, Kennedy. And I pulled these two photo's off the wall of his office, take a look and see if you can recognize anyone in the background."

Walsh put the newspaper down and held one photo in each hand; he went back and forth between the two photos. He spent several minutes going from one photo to the next, when a light seemed to go off in his head and he slowly looked up smiling, "Well, I'll be damned. Agent Addler and old Leathernuts. What the hell are they all doing together, and with a couple of commie big shots?"

"That's what I'd like to know. We need to tread lightly, especially with Addler, until we can nose around ourselves, damn CIA, for all we know they could have this place bugged. We got Joey Rocco coming in this morning with his lawyer, let's see what he was to say, but let's keep what we know to ourselves."

"Got it."

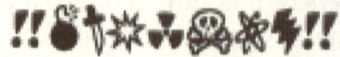

Roscoe and Jim were discussing how they were going to handle Rocco when LuJack from Robbery stuck his head into Brown's office, "Hey Roscoe, there's some grease ball hood and his Perry Mason are waiting for you downstairs."

"Thanks Tony."

The two detectives went downstairs to meet their guest and show them into interview room 3.

Roscoe and Jim sat on one side of the table and Joey and his attorney, Dominick DiCocco sat on the other side. Roscoe asked if either would like something to drink, they both declined.

"So, first let me say I appreciate you coming down and talking to us. You are not under arrest; we just have a couple of questions regarding Mr. Richard Moffit. We understand that you are a member of the United Hatters, Cap and Millinery Workers International Union, is that correct?"

"Yeah, I'm on the board."

"And in what capacity?"

"I'm the Vice-President of the central grievance committee."

"Have there been any grievances lately?"

Rocco get a big grin on his face, "Naw, not since I've been Vice-President, know what I mean?"

"We heard that you were thinking of running for President of the UHCMW, is that right?"

"Yeah, I was thinking of throwing my hat into the ring. I think I'd make a good President, ya know."

"How was your relationship with Mr. Moffit?"

"Whadda mean, relationship? You calling me some kinda brownie queen?"

"Take it easy, Joey. All I meant was how did you two get along, were you friends or did you have any beefs with the guy, that's all."

"Oh sorry, no we were solid. I liked "the Derby", he was a good Joe."

"We're asking everyone who knew Mr. Moffit, where were you yesterday between 9 am and 2 pm? For the record."

"Like I told you yesterday, I was at the Wimpy Boys Club. You can ask anyone, they'll tell you."

"Can you give me some names, it would make my life easier."

"Well let me see, there was Mikey "Two Guns" Marino, Tony "Fat Tuna" Esposito, Richard "the Boot" Barone, Carmine "the Grinder" Agosti, Vincent "Vinnie" De Luca, and Sammy "the Bull" Santoro."

"Wow, a virtual who's who of the underworld."

"Yeah, I only hang out with the cream de la cream."

"Have you, in your capacity as Vice President of the UHCMW done any traveling either inside or outside the United States with Moffit?"

"Yeah, we had some meetings with lots of high-class people, discussing union business, ya know."

"Where have you gone recently?"

"Why?"

"Look Joey, we're trying to figure out who might have wanted to kill Moffit, so we need to know who he had been in contact with. And since you guys had traveled together, you might know if anybody you met with might have had it in for Mr. Moffit either somebody here or maybe some foreign angle."

"Can't you just look up his travel itinerary?"

"Sure, but that just tells us where he went and who he met, it can't tell us how the meetings went and how the people got along with Moffit, you can give us the inside scoop."

"Hey, I ain't no rat!"

"Mr. DiCocco, a little help?"

Joey's lawyer leaned over and whispered in Joey's ear for a good five minutes, all the while Rocco was looking at Roscoe and nodding.

"Alright, alright, so, we met with Tommy "the Fox" DiNapoli, the local union head outta Chicago a couple of months ago, also in the U.S. we got together with Harry "the Horse" Warwick from Los Angeles, nice guy. Then we went over to Cuba, smoked a couple of them Cuban stogies and drank a lot of rum with that Fidel Castro, now that guy's a real nut, let me tell you."

"How did Moffit get along with Castro?"

"By the end of our stay, they were best buddies. Fidel signed a deal where the UHCMW was contracted to make all of their little green army caps for the next twenty years."

"Okay, and after Cuba?"

"Let's see, oh yeah we went to Moscow and met with that old shoe slammer, Nikita Khrushchev. Them Russkies call this guy "the Boss", nobody messes with this little prick."

"How did that go?"

"Old Khrushchev was like our new best friend, especially when we presented him with a specially made fedora made just for him, but he was really ragging on Johnny K for ruining the hat industry in America."

"What do you mean ruining the hat industry? Men still wear hats here."

"Yeah, not so much anymore. You haven't noticed? You look at the average Joe, not so much."

Walsh jumped in, "What a load of Commie crap."

"Hey, I'm just telling you what the old man said."

Roscoe asked, "Go anywhere else?"

"On the way back we stopped off in France. We met with that Frenchy de Gaulle, we got nowhere with that weasel. He wasn't impressed with the quality of our

American made berets, snob. And after all we did to save their ass from the Nazis, that's some gratitude."

"You in the war Joey?"

"Me, hell no!"

"So, Joey who all went on these trips with you?"

"Let me see, there was about six of us all toll, there was me, Dickie, Harold Brooks, Larry Page, Kevin McCarthy, and Lou Addler."

"And what is everyone's title?"

"Can't you just look it up?"

"Joey, you're sitting right here."

"Well okay, you know me and Dickie's title, ah Harold is Treasurer, Larry's the Secretary, Kevin is the Executive Vice President and Lou is the Sergeant at Arms."

"Well, we really want to thank you for being so cooperative and taking the time to come down here and hopefully help us find out who killed Dickie "the Derby" Moffit."

"Fuggedaboutit."

!! ☗†☼⚓☠�֍❖ !!

Betty was asleep on the sofa when he walked into the apartment, she was still in her pajamas from the morning, the television was on, but thankfully the sound was turned down. He leaned down and kissed her and ran his hand thru her long blond hair, she smiled and gave a low purring moan, "Mmmm, hi baby." She said with her eyes still closed.

"You promised that you were going to get out for some fresh air."

"I thought I'd wait for you and we could go for a walk together."

"Okay, go change."

They walked down 20th Avenue for several blocks to 86th Street until they reached Henry Wong's Chinese Restaurant. "Hey, how about some Chinese?" Roscoe asked.

"Sounds yummy, the usual?"

"Yeah, and I'll even spring for some egg rolls."

"Wow, big spender. Let's eat in, I don't feel like going back into the apartment right now."

They sat in the booth in the front window so they could watch the people walking by while they ate their, Moo Goo Gai Pan, Chop Suey, and steamed broccoli, with a side order of two egg rolls.

Afterward, they took their doggy bag of leftovers and walked down to Max & Mina's Ice Cream to share a double-dipped chocolate cone. They walked around the block slowly ten or twelve times until it got dark, then they headed up to Betty's apartment where Ajax, her calico cat was waiting not so patiently to be fed.

Roscoe and the cat usually got along okay, except when he would spend the night; Ajax wasn't too thrilled in having to share the bed with him and Betty. After they sat and talked awhile, about anything but the assassination they decided to go to bed. Roscoe and Betty cuddled for the longest time, she wanted to be held close and made to feel safe, nothing was making any sense, first, there was the Cuban Missile Crisis, which scared America to its very core. The world was so close to being blown up in a nuclear holocaust and now this.

They fell asleep in each other's arms and woke up when the cat tried to squeeze in between them at sunrise. Roscoe gingerly picked Ajax up, took him into the kitchen and fed him; he then went back into the bedroom where he and Betty made passionate love.

The phone rang, waking the two lovers from a deep and sound sleep. Roscoe quickly slipped on his boxer shorts and ran to the phone, catching a glance of the time, 5 a.m.

"Hello?"

"Roscoe, it's Jim. We got a murder."

"Who?"

"Delores Moffit."

"Where are you?"

"Manhattan."

"Why aren't they handling it?"

"They knew we were on the Moffit case and figured it was related."

"Okay, where are you?"

"Fifty-seventh and Sixth Avenue. She was gunned down in front of the Horn & Hardart Automat."

"I'll be there as soon as I can."

"Forty-five minutes later Detective Brown pulls up to the crime scene, there must have been close to thirty cops milling around doing nothing but taking up space. The coroner had already taken the body away; all that was left was the chalk outline of Mrs. Moffit on the sidewalk with an enormous bloodstain that had flowed all the way to the gutter. Walsh was talking to an elderly man inside the restaurant when Roscoe arrived; he nodded an acknowledgment when he saw him enter. Roscoe approached when Walsh thanked the man and let him go.

"Whatda we got?"

"Well the perps weren't shy, they were outside standing on the corner waiting for her to come out and when she did two guys opened fire, shooting her twelve times. According to eyewitnesses, there were three of them, two shooters and a backup. Afterward, a car pulled up and they all got in and drove away. Of course, no one got the license plate number, it was a dark-colored Ford sedan, four-door. They all wore dark overcoats, hats, gloves, and nobody got a good look at these punks, it all happened so fast and people were ducking for cover. So basically, we got bupkis."

"Well, it sounds like they were sending a message to someone. I'm sure our little pal Leatherballs either knows or had something to do with this. Has the crime lab gathered up any evidence, which I don't guess there is any, and since they used revolvers there aren't any shell casings, so you're right we got bupkis."

Roscoe stood looking around at the macabre circus all around him, he called for the uniformed sergeant to come over, "Sergeant you can send everyone home, there's nothing more we can do here. Thank you and your men for all your help."

As everyone started to disperse, police, crowd, and witnesses, one of the restaurant's employees brought out a hose and started washing Delores Moffit's blood off the sidewalk down into the gutter.

Roscoe turned to Walsh and said, "Have you eaten? I'm starved. Let's go inside and grab some breakfast."

Roscoe walked up to the bank guard.

"May I help you sir?"

"Yes, I'd like to see the bank manager." Roscoe said as he flashed his shield.

"Certainly sir, please follow me." The elderly bank guard said.

The guard led Roscoe to the manager's office located in the back of the bank. The guard announced Roscoe, "Excuse me Mr. Wilson, there's a Detective Brown to see you sir."

The manager, Mr. Wilson looked like a caricature of the bank manager from the board game Monopoly, fat, large mustache, balding wearing a pinstriped suit. "Come in Detective, how may I assist you?"

"Well sir, I'm investigating the murder of a Mr. Richard Moffit who has leased a safety deposit box with you folks and I need to open it."

"I see." He reached over and pressed a button on the intercom and spoke into the large box, "Marge, could you see what we have on a Mr. Richard Moffit?"

"Yes, Mr. Wilson right away." A tinny voice spewed out of the box.

"Ah, please have a seat Detective." Wilson said gesturing for Roscoe to have a seat in one of the plush chairs opposite the bank manager.

"Thank you, sir."

"A murder investigation, you say?"

"That's right, Richard Moffit, the President of the United Hatters, Cap and Millinery Workers International Union."

"Hmm, don't think I ever met the man, pity."

There was a knock on the door and a middle-aged woman wearing a tweed blazer and matching skirt, her hair was up in a bun and she wore eyeglasses that looked like the bottom two Coke bottles, she had the appearance of an owl.

"Here's the file for Richard Moffit, Mr. Wilson."

"Thank you Marge, that will be all."

She smiled and nodded, then left the room. Brown noticed the subtle looks they exchanged with each other and knew that they were lovers.

"Well, Detective Brown it looks that Mr. Moffit had rather substantial savings account with us as well as the safety deposit box."

Roscoe held out his hand and asked, "May I see that, sir?"

The bank manager passed the account file over to Detective Brown who was surprised at the amount that was in the account, over eight hundred thousand dollars. He looked at Wilson; "I'll need a copy of this, as soon as possible."

"No problem, I'll have my secretary make one for you while I take you down to inspect the safety deposit box if that's alright?"

"That will be fine, may I leave my hat and briefcase here, Mr. Wilson?"

"Yes, of course."

Wilson handed the account file to his secretary as they passed by her desk, he told her that Brown needed a copy as soon as possible and that they would be right back.

The safety deposit box vault was located downstairs of the bank next to their walk-in International Vault, that held the bank's cash reserve holdings of over fourteen million dollars in cash and gold bullion. Three armed guards were stationed outside of the vaults, with another two armed guards seated inside the main vault. In the past twenty-five years, there had only been one attempted robbery and that resulted in the robbers being shot dead before they even reached the vault's massive doors.

Mr. Wilson found Moffit's box and with his key and the one provided by Detective Brown, Wilson retrieved the box and showed Roscoe into a private viewing room where he left the Detective alone.

The box was a large one, measuring 35 inches high, 40 inches wide and 22 inches deep. When he opened it there was eights sealed 12X15 brown catalog envelopes each filled with fifty-thousand dollars cash, lying under the envelopes were four passports, one U.S. and three foreign all with Moffit's picture, but all with different aliases. A Russian passport showed him as Boris Kuznetsov, in a Brazilian one he was Fabrizio Oliveria, and an Egyptian passport had him under the name of Rashida Ghannam. Beneath the envelopes and passports there was a loaded .38 Smith & Wesson revolver and finally, on the very bottom of the safety deposit box wrapped in a black cloth was a framed photograph that left New York City Detective Sergeant Roscoe Brown gobsmacked and weak in the knees.

After forty minutes Mr. Wilson knocked on the door and asked, "Is everything alright Detective?"

As Roscoe opened the door he handed the box back to the bank manager and said, "Fine. I'm taking these few items with me. I've made a list of what I'm taking. I'm giving you a copy of the items I'm bringing with me."

He handed Wilson the list, Wilson perused it, and mumbled, "Four passports and a framed photograph. Very good, is there anything else that I can help you with?"

"Just the copy of Moffit's account file and, no one is to access this safety deposit box. Here's my card, if anyone, and I mean anyone contacts you, call me immediately, understand?"

"Yes, Detective."

"I don't care if Jesus Christ comes down from Heaven himself, no one."

"Yes sir, I understand."

They went back upstairs to the bank manager's office and retrieved the copy of Moffit's savings account file and placed it and the things from the safety deposit box in his briefcase.

!! 💀†☆☂💀☠⚡!!

Roscoe walked out of the Mechanics & Traders Bank in a bit of a daze. As he was walking to his car, he noticed two shadowy figures sitting in a black sedan parked on the opposite side of the street. He had seen them parked there when he entered the bank earlier, something wasn't Jake. He stopped and acted like he had forgotten something and went back into the bank. He reappeared after a few minutes and headed to his car.

When he got into the car he undid the snap on his shoulder holster, placed the briefcase on the seat next to him and drove off towards the station. He was aware that the car in front of him was driving suspiciously and the car behind him had the two guys from across the bank in it.

He was boxed in, at an intersection the two hoods in the car behind him jumped out and ran up to his car. The man on his left put a gun to Roscoe's head while the other one on the passenger side grabbed the briefcase. The man with the gun said, "Don't try anything stupid, copper."

The light changed and the two cars were gone leaving him stopped in the middle of the street with cars blasting their horns. Roscoe took off to the 60th Precinct and was cautiously observing if he was being followed, he wasn't.

When he parked in front of the station he took the items that he had removed from his briefcase back at the bank and had stuffed inside his suit jacket up to his office and place them into his office safe, locked it and went and got Walsh.

"Hey Jimmy, got a minute?"

"Sure thing, what's up?"

They walked back to his office, Roscoe let Walsh lead them into the room after they were in Roscoe locked the door. He walked over to his safe, opened it up and took out the framed photograph still wrapped in the black cloth. Roscoe stood in front of Walsh trying to gather his thoughts before he spoke.

Walsh could see that something heavy was on Roscoe's mind, "What is it Roscoe, what is it?"

"I don't know if I should show you this."

"What? What is it?"

"Okay, but you've got to swear to God that you won't tell anybody what I'm going to show you."

"Okay."

"Swear it."

"I swear it. You're really scaring me Roscoe, what is it?"

Roscoe unwrapped the cloth to reveal a black and white candid group photo of Dickie Moffit, Joey Rocco, CIA Agent Lou Addler and Lee Harvey Oswald taken in August 1963 at a pro-Castro rally in New Orleans sitting together smiling, just four months before Oswald killed Kennedy.

"Holy Mother of God!" Walsh whispered.

There was a knock on the door, "Hey you guys come out here quick!" Detective Davis shouted.

"Be right out!" Roscoe said as he quickly locked the photo back into his safe.

As they entered the squad room Walsh asked, "What's going on?"

Everyone in the squad room was glued to the small black and white television in the corner.

"At 1:20p.m. November 24th Eastern Standard Time, in the basement of the Dallas police station, Lee Harvey Oswald, the alleged assassin of President John F. Kennedy, was shot to death by Jack Ruby, a Dallas nightclub owner."

Roscoe and Walsh stunned, looked at each other in silence and went back into Roscoe's office and sat without saying a word, each deep in thought. Until Roscoe told Walsh about the stickup at the stoplight.

"Jesus, Roscoe who were those guys?"

"It had to be the Mafia or the CIA or both. But, by now they know I still have the photo. Betty!"

"Betty?"

"Yeah, these guys won't stop at nothing to get that photo, that's why they probably killed Mrs. Moffit and they can threaten me with Betty to get it, I got to warn her."

Roscoe jumped up and closed his door and picked up the receiver and called her at the bank.

"Hello, this is Detective Brown of the 60th precinct, I need to speak with Miss Armstrong. Yes, I'll hold."

He held his hand over the receiver and said to Walsh, "Go get the Captain, no wait. Hello Betty, I don't have time to explain, but you may be in danger, I need you to stay there don't go anywhere, I'll be by in a half hour. I'll explain when I get there, now go, and baby be careful. I love you."

Roscoe hung up the phone and was headed out the door when Walsh stopped him, 'Roscoe, shouldn't we tell the Captain?"

"When I get back, we'll tell him everything."

"Anything I can do"

"Stay close to the phone I might need you."

Roscoe arrived at the Maspeth Savings Bank, he parked in front by a fire hydrant, turned down the driver's side sun visor that had a piece of cardboard attached by two rubber bands with the word POLICE printed on it, locked the car and jogged inside.

Betty was behind the cashiers counter helping a young mother, who was struggling with her two children that were acting rowdy. He got in line behind the woman, tipped back his hat and peered down at the rambunctious kids sternly, then gave a short cough to get their attention, he showed the kids his badge, the result was that of total compliance and decorum and the rest of the transaction was completed quickly.

He stepped up to the counter and said, "Betty, we got to go now. Go get your things while I talk to the manager."

She placed the "next teller" please sign in her window and went into the back to get her purse and coat, while Roscoe went to talk to see Mr. Hoffman, the manager to give him the Readers Digest version of what was going on."

Betty came into the lobby and Roscoe took her arm and escorted her to the car. Once he had pulled away he told her that he had obtained a crucial piece of evidence in his murder case of Richard Moffit and some bad people were trying to get it, and he feared that they might try to get it by either threatening her or maybe even hurting her, so he had to get her away.

"Where we going?"

"I already talked to your brother Jack and we agreed that you'd be safe with them in Massapequa."

"Roscoe, I'm scared."

"No need babe, everything is going to be alright. I'm really close to solving the case and once I do, everything will be fine. I promise."

!! 🌑☨☆⚓☠✳⚡!!

Ten minutes after Detective Brown and Betty left the Maspeth Savings Bank, three armed men wearing dark overcoats, hats, gloves and holding revolvers walked into the bank and demanded all the money in the safe and forcing all the tellers and bank personnel to lie down on the floor in the lobby. Mr. Hoffman had the presence of mind to trip the silent alarm and the police and FBI were there within minutes and had surrounded the bank.

The hostage negotiator, Detective Tommy Herons called into the bank trying to establish a rapport with the robbers. They told the police that if they weren't allowed to leave unharmed and with the money that they would start throwing bodies out every fifteen minutes, starting with one Betty Armstrong.

The leader of the bank robbers, Benedetto "Benny Blue Eyes" Amatto shouted out, "All right where's Betty Armstrong!"

Nobody moved, then he shouted out again, "I said, where is Betty Armstrong? Don't make me ask again!"

Mr. Hoffman lifted his head and said, "Betty had to leave early, she wasn't feeling well."

This did not sit well with Benny Blue Eyes, "God Damnit!"

Sammy "Smoots" Guglielmetti and Joseph "Joey Dogs" Tagliagamba gathered with Benny and had to reevaluate the situation, the whole purpose of the robbery was to be able to put the whack on this Armstrong broad without making it look intentional. Being able to think on the fly wasn't the strong suit of any of these three, the three of them thinking as hard as they could, couldn't figure out how to fry an egg.

Smoots' wanted to whack all the hostages and try blasting their way out, Joey Dogs thought they might be able to try and tunnel their way out to the building next door and sneak out when it got dark, but they decided to go with Benny Blue Eyes plan, surrender. He figured that they would only be charged with attempted armed robbery and kidnapping, but no murder charges.

So, they'd do a long stretch in the joint, they were all made men, no one's going to mess with them. Plus, the bosses told them that the organization would look after their families while they were gone and when they got out there would be a hundred thousand bonus waiting for them if they did get out. As everyone knows, shit happens in prison and the odds that these three jamokes making it out alive were stacked against them, the bosses would see to that, after all, they didn't even get the job done, the bums, so screw 'em.

The ride back from dropping Betty off with her brothers was uneventful, by the time he got back into the city and to the station, Walsh was waiting for him.

"Roscoe, thank God you got Betty out when you did, I don't know if you heard, but three hoods went in an tried to rob the Maspeth Savings Bank, it was pretty clear that it was just a ruse so that they could either kill Betty or at least hold her hostage so you'd give them what they want."

"Was anyone hurt?"

"No, after they realized that she wasn't there, they played for time and made a good showing for the bosses, then they eventually gave themselves up."

"Is the Captain around?"

"No, he went home for the day. Want that we should call him at home?"

"No, it can wait until tomorrow. I'm thinking that since they don't know Betty is out of town they'll still try and pull something. You got any plans for this evening?"

"No, nothing planned."

"You up for a little adventure?"

"Always, what did you have in mind?"

!!�☜☀⚡!!

Betty's apartment was pitch black at 3 a.m. when Joey "Leathernuts" Rocco and Vinnie "Whack-Whack" Giuliani picked the lock and entered. They stood in the foyer letting their eyes get used to the darkness. They tiptoed into the living room to find all the blinds were closed, again they stood silently still trying to adjust to the blackness the engulfed them.

"I told you we should have brought a flashlight, Joey." Vinnie whispered.

"Fuggedaboutit."

Roscoe had been sitting on the sofa since midnight in the dark waiting. He sat quietly holding his loaded Smith & Wesson Model 10 revolver; his eyes had adjusted to the minimal amount of light that allowed him to see the two figures standing less than ten feet away from him. He reaches up with his left hand and switched on the floor lamp next to him.

When the light came on Roscoe saw Joey holding a Beretta .22LR pistol with a silencer and his partner carrying a sawed-off Remington pump-action shotgun. Whack-Whack's body was slightly turned away from Roscoe, so when the lights came on his natural reaction was to swing the shotgun around and start blasting. Unfortunately for Whack-Whack, Roscoe had his revolver up and pointed at the two of them, he fired one shot hitting Vinnie in the throat, causing him to drop his shotgun and cartwheel backward spraying the room with spurts of blood as he fell to the floor. Roscoe pointed the gun to Leathernuts who dropped his pistol and held his hands up pleading, "Don't shoot, copper I give up."

Joey stood motionless with his hands up in the air covered in Whack-Whack's blood. Vinnie lay dying emitting a gurgling frothing sound as his carotid artery spouted blood into the air until he eventually bled out giving a final exhale of air, then nothing.

Roscoe stood up from the sofa and was reaching behind his back for his handcuffs when Joey's head exploded from a gunshot coming from the foyer, his blood and brains comingled with Whack-Whacks on the wall and window blinds. As Roscoe started to react, in from the entrance way walked CIA Agent Lou Addler pointing his gun at Detective Brown, "Put the gun down Detective Brown, I don't want to kill you but I will."

Roscoe did as he was told; he placed his gun on the coffee table in front of him. Addler walked over and picked up Roscoe's revolver off the coffee table and said, "Have a seat, let's talk."

Agent Addler sat down in the armchair across from the sofa, pointing the gun at Brown. "Where is she?"

"Betty's not here."

"Good. That would just complicate matters."

Addler looked at the two dead hoods bleeding on the carpet. "Boy, what a mess, you know you'll never get those stains out, you're going to need new carpet."

"Yeah, somehow I think that's going to be the least of my worries."

"I told these goombahs it wasn't going to be easy, but no, they tell me, Lou, it's going to be simple, badda bing badda boom."

"Well, I don't know about badda bing, but there sure was a lot of badda boom."

"Yeah, now Roscoe, may I call you Roscoe?"

"You're holding the gun."

"Right, now Roscoe where's the photo? You give me that photo and I'm outta here and you and Betty can go live happily ever after."

"Maybe, but I'm thinking that once I give you the photo I'll be lying there next to old Leathernuts and his buddy."

"Whack-Whack."

"What?"

"That's the other guy bleeding on your carpet, Vinnie "Whack-Whack" Giuliani."

"They have such colorful names, Whack-Whack."

"Look, I just want the photo."

"We both know that's not what's going to go down here, I'm not stupid, but I got to know why the CIA, the Mafia, the UHCMW, and an American communist nut job conspired to kill the President of the United States. I got to know. Consider it the last wish of dying man."

Addler sat holding the gun at Roscoe thinking and said, "Fair enough, but you know after I tell you, I will have to kill you."

"I got to know."

"It all started because the people at the UHCMW were convinced that JFK single-handedly killed the hat industry by being the first President not to wear a hat to his inauguration."

"Sure he did, he wore a top hat."

"Oh sure, he wore the top hat on the way to the ceremony alright, but then he removed it before addressing the crowd and taking the oath, remember? The hat industry started to decline shortly after Kennedy's promotion to the Oval Office, prompting many in the executive board to believe that he was the cause."

"But men still wear hats."

"Yeah, not so much anymore. You haven't noticed? Look around pal; maybe one in ten men today wear a hat. No, the hat industry is on the way out."

"Okay, but what about the mob?"

"Well, they got their panties in a wad when JFK appointed his brother Bobby as the U.S. Attorney General, who once he took over to put together a team to combat organized crime and they went after the bosses with a vengeance."

"Okay, as demented and delusional their reasons are, I can kind of understand, but the CIA?"

"Three words. Bay of Pigs."

"You guys wanted Kennedy dead because of the botched attempt to overthrow Castro?"

"That is just the tip of the iceberg, my friend. After the failed invasion, Kennedy was so mad about the failure that he said that he was stupid to trust the CIA and the Joint Chiefs of Staff and that he wanted to splinter the CIA into a thousand pieces and scatter it into the winds. We just couldn't stand by and watch that happen."

"And Lee Harvey Oswald?"

"We had been watching him for over two years, he was just malleable enough and dumb enough to be molded into believing that he was going to be received as a national hero, the poor sucker."

"Jack Ruby?"

"Well, we couldn't have Oswald spilling his guts and implicating the "Company" now could we? We had a bunch of stuff on Ruby that could make his life a living Hell, so we told him if he tapped Oswald good things would happen for his family and eventually we'll see that he gets released."

"But, I still don't understand how it all fell into place, you are all so different."

"It was like the perfect storm, Moffit was my next door neighbor, he was always bitching about Kennedy destroying the hat industry, and within the union, there was Joey Rocco, a known mobster and of course Oswald was the CIA's contribution to the party. So, one night over at Dickie's house the three of us were sitting around having drinks and getting rather shitfaced when, I think it was Leathernuts said, "You know what, somebody should kill that son of a bitch Kennedy." And that's how it all started, it kind of had a life of its own once it got rolling and it continued to pick up speed."

"Moffit?"

"Yeah, in the end, he got cold feet, we couldn't risk him shooting his mouth off, plus he had that damn photograph. So, Whack-Whack did what his name implies, I gave him the copy of the house key that Dickie had given me, as good neighbors tend to do, and he found Moffit sitting at his desk with his back to Vinnie. The rest is how you say, history."

"But why kill Mrs. Moffit?"

"Ah, that was all Rocco, he thought she might know where the photo was and when it was clear she didn't, Whack-Whack."

"Did it go higher up in the Company, or were you a lone wolf?"

"It was me and Director of Mission Resources and Operations Robert Mulligan. We didn't do it for glory, but to save the Company. Now, is there anything else you'd like to know?"

"No. What an amazing story, no one would ever believe it."

"Okay, Detective Brown, where is the photo?"

"It's in the safe in my office."

It was at that moment when CIA Agent felt the barrel of Detective James Walsh's Smith & Wesson Model 10 pressed against the back of his head.

"Drop the gun Agent Addler and don't try anything or there will be your brains on the wall along with Rocco's." Walsh said in a low confident voice.

Addler did as he was told.

"Now stand up a place your hands behind your back."

Roscoe took the handcuffs that he was going to place on Leathernuts, but instead put them on Addler.

"Did you get all that?" Roscoe asked Walsh.

"Let's see." Jim said as he pressed the rewind button on the tape recorder that they had set up earlier. Garbled sounds from the whirling rewinding tape had a morbid comedic cartoon tone that somehow seems to punctuate the grisly scene that surrounded them.

"Okay press play."

"It was like the perfect storm, Moffit was my next door neighbor, he was always bitching about Kennedy destroying the hat industry, and within the union, there was Joey Rocco a known mobster and of course Oswald was the CIA's contribution to the party. So, one night over at Dickie's house the three of us were sitting around having drinks and getting rather shitfaced when, I think it was Leathernuts said, "You know what, somebody should kill that son of a bitch, Kennedy." And that's how it all started, it kind of had a life of its own once it got rolling and it continued to pick up speed."

"Okay Addler, let's go." Roscoe said as he nudged the CIA agent to get moving.

"Where are you taking me?"

"You're under arrest."

"For what?"

"Well for one thing, how about the murder of Whack-Whack and Joey "Leathernuts" Rocco."

"What those punks, I should get a medal."

"Come on let's go."

!! 🔥 🗡 ✵ ☙ 💀 ✺ ⚡ !!

The honorable Mayor Richard F. Wagner Jr. of New York City sat at the head of the table and sitting on either side was John A. McCone head of the CIA, Louis J. Lefkowitz the New York State Attorney General, New York City Police Commissioner Raymond Kelly, finally, the Captain of the 60th Precinct Captain Sean O'Rourke, and bringing up the rear was Detectives Brown and Walsh.

"Gentlemen, I am at a loss for words." Mayor Wagner declared.

McCone head of the CIA said, "This must never get out, this would tear at the very fabric of our country that so desperately in the process of trying to come to grips with such a devastating loss."

"What should we do, sweep it under the rug? There all kinds of legal implications such a cover-up would create. Can you imagine what would happen if we tried to cover this up and it got out to the public, chaos!" Lefkowitz proclaimed.

"Detective Brown, is this the only copy of the tape?" McCone asked.

"No sir, I have made a copy of the tape and along with the original photograph, that I have secured away with specific instructions that if anything were to happen to myself, Detective Walsh or my fiancée then these items would be released to the media. Detective Walsh and I have no intention of releasing any of these pieces of evidence, but we feel that having them in our figurative possession, considering the explosive nature of them is the only way to keep us safe. I must tell you that Betty Armstrong, my fiancée has zero knowledge of this matter what's so ever, but she was made a target so as to get to me."

"And what if we compel you to turn them over to us?" McCone inquired.

"With all due respect sir, you do what you have to and we'll do the same."

"You know Detective Brown, Detective Walsh if for any reason any of this gets out heads will roll."

"Mr. McCone, if any of this gets out more than just our heads will roll." Brown retorted.

Mayor Wagner stood up, "So it's agreed. McCone, you have the tape, gentlemen let's conclude this meeting that never happened."

As they were walking out of the Mayor's office Roscoe caught up to the CIA Director and asked, "Mr. McCone, I have a question, what's going to happen to Agent Addler?"

"Addler, Addler? Never heard of him."

Roscoe and Walsh were sitting in Brown's office decompressing when Walsh asked, "Roscoe did we do the right thing? You know two wrongs don't make a right."

"That's true Jimmy, but three rights make a left."

The Case of the Devil's Bite

Lucifer the cat would sit looking out the upstairs apartment window every day, watching the people yell, scream, and laugh as they rode the Astroland Cyclone Rollercoaster located across the street. The apartment sat above Julio's International Spanish & American Grocery store at 1013 Surf Avenue and faced the Astroland Amusement Park. The subway ran right behind the building if you opened the bedroom window you could touch the elevated tracks that led to the West 8th Street, Surf Avenue & New York Aquarium stop. It was a good thing the old lady; Mrs. Stieferman that lived in apartment three was hard of hearing.

Mrs. Stieferman and her husband Klaus had lived there for over fifty years, so when Mr. Stieferman died two years ago, Mrs. Stieferman decided to stay, after all this was her home. Where would she go? They had no children, just Lucifer.

Lucifer was an orange tabby that wandered into their open bedroom window one day from the subway tracks and decided to stay and adopt the old man and his wife twelve years ago. Lucifer weighed fifteen pounds, had piercing greens eyes, a shiny carrot colored coat, and one snaggle tooth. When looking at his left silhouette, he looked like a regular cat, but from the right profile, because his right canine tooth was almost twice as long as his left, he looked like a sabertooth tiger.

The old couple would put Lucifer in a baby carriage and take long walks up and down the boardwalk. They would sit on a bench along the walk overlooking the beach and just sit there and spend hours watching the people on the beach, Lucifer would watch, too, but mostly the feline would just lay in the carriage and sleep. Occasionally, people would stop by and want to pet the nice kitty, which they allowed, that is if Lucifer approved of them. Sometimes people would give the old couple a few dollars to help feed the sweet kitty.

Now that Klaus had passed, there would be times when Mrs. Stieferman and Lucifer would eat dinner out of the same can. Klaus had been a very successful shoe repairman, he had his shop downstairs, but after his stroke, he had to let the shop go and Julio took over and turned it into a grocery store. With what little social security that they received, rent and utilities took most of that, what was left went to food. Winters were especially hard; the heating bills took up a lot of her meager monthly check, so during the winter months she and Lucifer would share cans of Friskies Meaty Bits, Pate, Tasty Treasures with real bacon, but their favorite was Prime Filets. Mrs. Stieferman would occasionally go over to Lenny's Deli and have a cup of chicken noodle soup and bring home a dozen or so packages of soda crackers, which she would have with the Friskies.

Julio liked the old lady and would give her any of the old fruit or vegetables that he couldn't sell, and sometimes when the homemade chili that had sat in the pot for over a week and was baked on to the bottom of the pot, he would scrape it into a paper cup and take it upstairs to her, it figured it was better than eating cat food.

The Coney Island Boys is a famous New York City street gang that came together sometime around the 1950s. Their turf stretched from Seagate, Brighton Beach to Manhattan Beach. These model citizens of the community are involved in assaults, drug trafficking, bookmaking, extortion with an occasional murder.

Late one August night Mrs. Stieferman heard a loud ruckus coming from the store below, she quietly tiptoed down the stairs that led to the back entrance of Julio's grocery. She hid behind some boxes in the storeroom and saw several young men pushing and hitting Julio, one man hit him so hard that he knocked him down. She heard one of them yell, "Listen spic, either you pay us a hundred dollars a week or you're going to find windows broken and maybe even a fire. You dig you freaking greaser?"

Julio said nothing, he was grabbed by two of the thugs and forced to open the cash register.

"We're taking two hundred bucks grease ball, think of it as the first and last installment, right Shaggy?"

"Yeah, right Psycho."

"We'll be back next Friday, and you better have the dough."

As they walked out laughing, they each grabbed a handful of candy bars.

After they left Mrs. Stieferman came into the store, "Are you alright Julio?"

Julio picked up a rag from behind the counter and wiped the blood from his cut lip. He turned to her in embarrassment said, "I'm fine Mrs. Stieferman, it's just some neighborhood punks shaking me down for extortion money, a hundred dollars a week. I can't afford that, I don't know what I'm going to do."

"You can call the police."

"If I do, I can tell you what will happen, the police will come out and talk to those punks and they'll leave me alone for a couple weeks or months and then they'll come back and beat me up or kill me. No, Mrs. Stieferman I don't think calling the police is a good idea."

"Well, you have to do something, Julio."

"I will Mrs. Stieferman, I will. I thank you for your concern, now go on up and tend to Lucifer."

"Are you sure there isn't anything I can do?"

"I'm sure. Good night."

"Good Night."

!! 🕯✝☆⚡☠✳⚡!!

Detective Roscoe Brown had just walked into Nathans Famous Hot Dogs on the boardwalk and saw his old friend, Vinnie the counterman.

"Yo Vinnie, the usual."

"Listen Roscoe, you don't have to tell me every time you come in here that you want the usual. Two chilidogs, an order of crinkle cut French fries, and a cup of Joe, black is all you ever order, it's all you've ever ordered. For over ten years you come in here every day about this time and say, "Yo Vinnie, the usual."

"Well, excuse me for living."

"Here, here's your usual."

"Thanks."

"So, how's Betty?"

"She's terrific. Hey, did I tell you we're getting married next June."

"No, congratulations. Next June, huh? Maybe you should want us to cater it, I'll give you a great deal."

"Yeah thanks, I'll definitely talk it over with Betty."

"Yeah, think about it.

"Okay. You know it's such a beautiful day, I think I'm going to eat out on the boardwalk."

"Okay, so I'll see ya tomorrow."

Roscoe took the two chili dogs, fries, and coffee and sat down on one of the benches look out at the ocean. There was such a nice ocean breeze blowing that he took off his suit jacket. He had finished off both chilidogs and was polishing off his fries when an elderly lady pushing a baby carriage with a cat came and asked, "Excuse me, may I sit down?"

"Yes of course."

She sat down and without looking at him asked, "Are you a police officer?"

"Yes ma'am, I'm Detective Brown. How did you know?"

"I saw the badge on your belt when you sat down, is that alright?"

"Yes ma'am."

"My name is Mrs. Stieferman, and I live over on Surf Avenue above Julio's International Spanish & American Grocery store, do you know it?"

"No ma'am, not off hand."

"It's right across from the Cyclone rollercoaster."

"Is there a problem, Mrs. Stieferman?"

"Well Detective Brown, my friend Julio who owns the store was beaten up last night by a bunch of ruffians and they're demanding that he pay them a hundred dollars a week or else."

"Did your friend call the police?"

"No, he fears that calling the police would only make matters worse."

"What would you like me to do?"

"I don't know."

"Well, I could have a patrol car keep an eye on the store, that might help. But unless Julio comes to us for help, there's not much we can do."

I understand Detective, I thank you for listening to me."

"It was my pleasure and I wish there was more that I could do."

"I don't know if this helps but I heard them call each other by their names."

"Please tell me and I can look them up in our database."

"One was called Shaggy and the other one who seemed to be the leader was called Psycho."

"Shaggy and Psycho. That could help a lot Mrs. Stieferman. If I find anything out I'll contact you. What's your phone number?"

"Oh, I don't have a phone, too expensive. I used to have one when my husband was alive, but I have no use for one now."

"Well, Mrs. Stieferman if I find out anything I'll stop by and let you know. And if you don't mind my saying, your cat has a very unusual look, with that elongated tooth of his, he reminds me of a sabertooth tiger."

"Lucifer gets that a lot. Maybe that's why I love him so because he's not perfect."

"Right, but then again Mrs. Stieferman, who is."

!!☗†☼☆⚓☠✺⚡!!

When Roscoe got back to the 60th Precinct, he stopped by the gang unit and asked Detective Molinar if he knew of a gang member named and Psycho.

"Psycho, I know a dozen punks named Psycho."

"Well, what about Shaggy?"

"Sure, Shaggy and Psycho, they're a couple of the Coney Island Boys. In fact, Psycho is the gang leader. What's up?"

"I met an elderly woman who witnessed these punks shaking down a store owner. He's too scared to go to the police."

"Want us to have a little talk with these juvenile delinquents?"

50

"Only if you don't implicate any of the store owners."

"No problem, we'll make it look like a routine roust."

"Thanks, Molinar."

Roscoe went upstairs to his office in homicide where his partner James Walsh was waiting.

"Where ya been, Roscoe?"

"Why, we got a new murder that I haven't heard about?"

"You wish. No, the Captain wants you to finish up the report on the Jackson case."

"Got it right here, do you want me to bring it to him or do you want the brownie points?"

"Oh no, you can have all the glory."

"Thanks." Roscoe said as he left the office, halfway out the door he turned and said, "For nothing."

!!☀†✷⁂☠✳⚡!!

Johnny Laskow had been in and out of prison most of his life for assault, robbery, burglary, and rape. Johnny thought of himself as a Pink Panther style cat burglar, but in reality, he was just your basic second story man. He would break into people's homes and steal whatever he could put into his pockets. He wasn't the dashing suave burglar of high society, Laskow was a criminal of opportunity, he'd look for doors that weren't locked, windows that were left open, garage doors left up, especially at night, or cars with open windows. He was known as a snatch and grab thief, but if he had to use muscle he would, He carried a 12" lead pipe with a rubber bicycle grip handle for better holding when smashing a victims protesting arm. He felt he was justified hitting his mark if they pissed him off by resisting.

Johnny was casing several possibilities for his next "job" there was a parking lot near the Coney Island Amusement Park, always good for a bobble or two and easy to get lost in the boardwalk crowd. He had noticed that the auto body shop workers over on Mermaid Avenue had a nasty habit of leaving tools out for easy pickings when things got busy or when they took their lunch break. And then there was the apartment building next to the elevated subway tracks, he had spotted an old babe, who had to be at least a thousand years old, she would leave her bedroom window open at night this time of year when the weather was hot and humid, but because the apartment was near the water a nice breeze would cool things down. Johnny planned to have a date with Grandma Moses after dark, one of these nights when it pickings were thin.

Laskow's latest day of thievery was pretty much a bust, he only managed to grab two transistor radios from the parking lot and a ball-peen hammer from the body shop, after he pawned them he barely had enough for hamburger, fries and chocolate shake at McDonalds. Johnny wasn't in a good mood, the old lady had better come across with the goods. He needed a good score; after all he had expenses, being a thief wasn't cheap.

Detective Molinar and his partner Bill Campbell headed out to Astroland Amusement Park, home of the Coney Island Boys.

Astroland was built, like a space-age theme park when it opened 1962 since then it has become the base of operations for the goon squad known around Brooklyn as the Coney Island Boys. They could always be found hanging around the giant rocket ship sitting atop Gregory & Paul's concession stand, where people would lineup by the hundreds for knishes, pizzas, Italian sausages, hamburgers, hot dogs and of course ice cold beer. The Boys usually didn't mess around with the park's patrons except when they spotted an easy mark or someone that they thought maybe a queer.

The Coney Island Boys never ran from the cops like other gangs, they always stood their ground defying the authorities, proving to each other how tough they are. So, when Molinar and Campbell approached Psycho and his tribe they just sat casually at the picnic tables drinking their beers and eating their pizza.

"Listen up dirtbags. I've been hearing that some of yous have been naughty little boys. Going around threaten people, being rude and generally being a pain in the ass. So, me and Campbell here are telling you little shits that you better knock it off or I'll be forced to give you punks a leather shampoo, starting with you Harold."

"The name's Psycho, pig."

"Campbell, our little friend Harold wants to be called Psycho, he thinks it makes him a tough guy. That shit might work on Joe six-pack Harold, but don't mean shit to us. Just so you know we're keeping our eye on you little creeps."

"Ooh, you got me shaking in my boots, pig."

"Don't you mean booties, Harold? Come on Bill, let's go after some real criminals. Bye boys."

Molinar and Campbell drove back to the precinct and alerted the uniform patrol to be on the lookout for the Coney Island Boys getting into extortion of the local shop owners and to make their presence known.

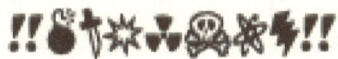

Roscoe and Betty were getting ready to leave Roscoe's apartment to go the movies to see Audrey Hepburn and Cary Grant in Charade when the phone rang.

"Hello, oh hi Jim. Where? Okay, I'll see you there as soon as I can."

Roscoe hung up the phone, "That was Jimmy."

"Don't tell me, there's been a murder."

"I'm sorry babe, maybe tomorrow."

"Sure, tomorrow."

"Hey, tonight on TV there's the Jackie Gleason Show and the Defenders. You know you love the Great One. I have some Jiffy-Pop in the cabinet, pop some up and we'll watch something when I get back."

"Just go, I'll be fine. You be careful."

Roscoe arrived at 1013 Surf Avenue a little after 7 p.m. and saw his partner, several uniformed police officers and the medical examiner standing outside Julio's International Spanish & American Grocery store.

"Whatda he have?" he asked Walsh.

"It's pretty brutal, the old lady who lived above the store was found beaten to death by the store owner, looks like she may have been sexually assaulted as well."

"Jesus Fucking Christ! What the hell's wrong with people?"

They headed upstairs to apartment 3 when they entered the ME was examining her. She was laying on her stomach; her body was covered with black & blue bruises from her head to her toes. The creep hit her so hard that he split the back of her head open.

When the doctor turned her over, Roscoe gasped, "I know this woman. It's Mrs. Stieferman; she's the one that I met on the boardwalk the other day. She's the one who told me about the punks who were extorting the storeowner downstairs. We need to talk to him."

Sitting on the windowsill was Lucifer watching all the strangers hovering around his master; he had seen the attack and was traumatized by it, to the point that he was on high alert. Nobody could approach him, he would hiss and arch his back in an attempt to let people know, don't even think about it, just back off! Eventually, they had to call animal control, Roscoe said that he wanted to take the cat back to his place because it was a possible witness or at least a piece of evidence. Animal control captured the sabertooth kitty and put him in a carrying case for Roscoe to take home. He brought along all the cat's belongings, his litter box, drinking, and food dish and some cat toys.

"When can you give us your report doc?"

"Tomorrow afternoon."

"Thanks doc."

Detective Walsh took Roscoe into the bedroom, "It looks like the perp might have climbed in from the subway tracks, the window was open when we got here, and there are no signs of forced entry. So, either she knew the guy or he came in thru the window."

"Let's have Molinar and Campbell check out these Coney Island Boys, they've been known to get a little rough with squealers and snitches. But, I can see them raping her and the beating was way over the top but have the boys in the gang unit do a follow up just in case."

"The boys from the crime lab have been and gone, so we'll see what if anything they come up with. They found a small amount of blood near the victim's body, so I'm hoping that it's the killers."

"Maybe Mrs. Stieferman scratched him, or could have been the cat, I'll stop by the lab on the way home so they check out his claws."

"Shall we go down and talk to Julio downstairs?" Walsh asked.

Roscoe and Walsh went downstairs after making sure all the windows and the front door was locked. Roscoe was carrying Lucifer in the carrier down with him and Walsh put the police seal on the door that forbids anyone entrance to the apartment, as it is still considered a crime scene.

"Where are you taking Lucifer?" Julio asked.

Roscoe placed the cat down and said, "I'm taking him with me for a while, he may have some of the evidence on him. Afterward, would you like him?"

"Sí por favor, yes please, with that crazy tooth he will make a great mouser."

"I'll make sure he is given to you, now tell me Mr.?"

"Gonzales."

"I am Detective Sergeant Brown and this is my partner Detective Walsh.

"Tell me Mr. Gonzales did you see anyone go upstairs to Mrs. Stieferman apartment tonight?"

"No, sir."

"Do you know of anyone who would want to hurt her?"

"Mrs. Stieferman, No, no everyone loved her and Lucifer too."

"I spoke to her on the boardwalk the other day about her witnessing an altercation between you and a couple gang members. She cared for you very much Mr. Gonzales and was worried. Can you tell me anything about that?"

"It was nothing, just a bunch of gamberros having mischief."

"Extortion is not mischief Mr. Gonzales. Do you think any of these gamberros might have seen her and hurt Mrs. Stieferman?"

"Dios ayúdame, maybe. I haven't seen them around in a couple of days."

"Would you be willing to come down and look at some mug shots and identify these gamberros?"

"Oh, I don't know."

"Look Mr. Gonzales, one of these little punks might have killed that dear old lady."

"Aprobado, I'll come down tomorrow morning."

"Thank you, we would appreciate your help, Mr. Gonzales. Walsh, can you think of anything else?"

Walsh asked, "Mr. Gonzales, did you hear any noise or disturbance upstairs?"

Julio walked over to the radio sitting on the counter next to the cash register and turned it on, music played. He said, "I have the radio on when I'm open, I never hear anything from upstairs. It would have had to be a real knock down and drag out fight for me to hear anything."

"I see, and who else lives in the other apartments upstairs?"

"I live in one of the apartments and the other is currently vacant."

Walsh closed up his notebook and looked at Brown and shrugged.

Roscoe picked up the cat carrier and he and Walsh walked out, Roscoe turned his head back towards Julio and said, "See you in the morning."

!! 🐾†✵☘︎☠︎☂︎⚡︎!!

By the time Roscoe got home Betty had gone to bed, the stop at the crime lab took longer than he thought it would. They check to see if the cat had any blood or human skin in or on his claws, they did not.

Roscoe set the carrier down while he set up Lucifer's litter box and food and water dishes, then he open the carrier door and walk over and sat on the sofa and waited. Lucifer peeked his head out of the wire door and slowly wandered out, he jumped up onto the living room windowsill and laid down. Roscoe got up turned off all the lights and went to bed. He snuggled up to Betty, who gave a soft moan and whispered with her eyes closed, "What time is it?"

"2 a.m."

"Everything okay?"

"Oh yeah, by the way, I brought home a cat, so don't be surprised when you see him."

"You brought home a cat?"

"He was the victim's cat and I had to take him into the lab for testing. I couldn't bring myself to have him stay in a shelter, so I brought him here for the night. His name is Lucifer and he's got this really long snaggle tooth, he's cute. I'm sure he saw the old lady get beaten to death and so he's a bit traumatized, so let him approach you."

Just then they felt a dip in the bed when Lucifer jumped on to the mattress, he wandered around the edge of the bed for a few minutes then curled up next to Betty and started to knead its paws against her body until she petted him. That's how Roscoe found them in the morning when he got up, Betty was lying on her right side in a fetal position with Lucifer fast asleep tucked in the curve of her body.

He showered, shaved, got dressed and went into the kitchen, plugged in the Sears Kenmore Percolator to make some Maxwell House coffee. He knew that the aroma of freshly brewed coffee would bring her around. He was working on his second cup of coffee sitting at the little table in the kitchen when Betty made her entrance and right behind her was her new best buddy, Lucifer.

"How did you sleep?" He asked.

"Like a rock and you?"

"Yeah, me too. I see that you and Lucifer have become fast friends."

"He's a cutie, I think we should adopt him."

"Maybe, I kinda promised him to the store owner where the old lady was living. He thinks he would be a good mouser, especially with that snaggle tooth."

"Oh no, he's too cute to be a mouser, besides we're pals, you said so yourself. Please?"

"Well, I'll have to tell Julio, the store owner."

Betty took Roscoe's hand and led him back into the bedroom.

"What's this?" He asked.

"Just my way of saying thank you."

"Maybe I should bring cats home more often."

"Shut up and get in bed."

!! 🔥†☆☀☠✳⚡!!

Johnny Laskow woke up with a massive hangover from drinking too much rum, what a night he had, all that time and effort for what? That old broad only had less than thirty bucks cash, the stuff he took and then hocked was worth a meager twenty-eight dollars.

Why did she have to resist, she should have just given him a blow job as he asked, but no. He tried to persuade her by giving her a few taps with the lead pipe, the more she resisted the harder the taps became. So, to punish her, he just had to rape her to show her that he was in charge and that she had to do as he said. That's how it works up in Attica.

While she was lying on the living room carpet naked, bleeding it dawned on him that if he didn't kill her, she would be able to identify him and he would go back to prison. And this time it would be forever, so she had to die.

Laskow let her lie there bleeding while he looked for something to eat, but all he found was six cans of cat food.

"Hey, old lady I'm hungry whadda got to eat? You better have something here more than just cat food or I'm going to get mad."

Mrs. Stieferman tried to say something but since he smashed her teeth out all she could do is mumble. He stomped over to where she lay and grabbed her by her hair and lifted her head, "What'd ya say?"

59

She managed to say, "There's some chili in the icebox."

"Chili, it better be good." He said and dropped her head like a sack of onions.

Johnny found the chili, ate it cold with the six packs of saltines, started to drink her only can of V8, then spit it out.

"Don't you have any liquor you old hag?"

She shook her head no, which only made him madder. He went back into the living room where she was lying on her back, he looked down at her and said, "You look like shit, bitch. I can't stand to look at you."

He took her by the arm and flipped her over, he took a pillow off of the couch and shoved it under her stomach, he undid his pants, dropped to his knees and raped her again. He was still on his knees when Lucifer walked over to his mistress; Laskow tried to grab the feline, that's when Lucifer glommed on Johnny's purlicue, the soft area between the forefinger and the thumb of his right hand, Lucifer latched onto it like a mousetrap snapping a rat's head.

"Motherfucker! I'm going to kill you, you little shit!" Johnny shouted as he tried to stand up and reach for his lead pipe, but he was having a hard time of it because his pants were around his ankles. As Johnny finally got to his feet Lucifer released his death grip and took off, leaving a perfect impression of his oddball bite mark and several drops of Johnny Laskow's blood on the floor.

Laskow was so enraged that he took his anger out on Mrs. Stieferman, hitting her so hard that he spit the back of her skull. "That'll teach you bitch, next time teach that little devil some manners."

He pulled up his pants, zipped up his fly, grabbed the pillowcase with all her personal possessions and left the way he came in, out the bedroom window.

Except for that damn cat, he thought he had a pretty good night. He would go and pawn this junk and buy a tall bottle of Bacardi Gold and celebrate.

!! 👊✝☼🔩💀✖⚡ !!

Roscoe got into the office an hour later than usual, but in a great mood, he was heard humming the Four Seasons smash hit "Walk Like a Man."

"What's with you?" Walsh asked.

"It's a beautiful day to catch a killer, but then again any day is a good day to catch a killer."

"How did Betty like the cat?"

"Oh, you mean Betty's new cat?"

"I hope Julio doesn't take it too hard."

"One can always get a mouser, but the perfect pet for my Betty, need I say more?"

Detectives Molinar stuck his head into Roscoe's office, "Bad news Brown, as far as your murder ID's concerned, the owner of Gregory & Paul's concession stand out at Astroland clams that the Coney Island punks were all there, all night, sorry."

"Yeah well, I knew that it couldn't be that easy. I guess we'll have to solve it the old fashion way, dumb luck. Thanks anyway."

"We won't hear back from the coroner until this afternoon. So, what do you want to do?" Walsh asked.

"Let's go back to the apartment, see if we missed anything last night. Things always look different in the daylight."

Standing inside Mrs. Stieferman apartment looking at the large bloodstain on the carpet where she was brutalized and killed things definitely looked different. The scene was even more barbarous and savage; Roscoe believed that he was dealing with a ravenous beast that was callous, apathetic and cold-blooded.

They looked around the apartment and went thru the drawers and cabinets and came across some photographs of her and Mr. Stieferman posing proudly wearing their finest clothes and jewelry, it looked to be either a birthday or wedding celebration. They took it and would check with the local pawnshops to see if anyone had pawned any jewelry that might match what she was wearing in the photograph.

Walsh re-examined the bedroom window and noticed that it appeared that someone had indeed "jimmied" the window to gain access. The intruder had left several distinctive marks from an unusual tool to break into Mrs. Stieferman's bedroom. Detective Walsh had brought along the squads Polaroid Land Camera and took several pictures to see if they could compare the marks left on the old lady's window to those of known thieves and robbers.

"Hey, Roscoe, take a look at these marks that the killer left on the window."

"What the hell could make a mark like that? Hopefully, the boys back in the lab might know what kind of tool would leave that kind of mark and the creep that used it. Nice work, Jimmy."

"Thanks, let's keep a good thought."

"Let's head back. Let's go out the back, I'm not ready to face Julio."

"Chicken."

"Cluck."

By the afternoon Laskow's hangover was gone, he was feeling high-spirited and lucky. He headed to the Astroworld auxiliary parking lot, it was a beautiful Saturday afternoon there would be hundreds of people going to the amusement park; the odds were in his favor that there would be a couple lazy, preoccupied or forgetful people that would leave something valuable in their unlocked car or one of the kids would forget to roll the window up. He could always count on the stupidity of people. People, you just had to love them.

Johnny couldn't believe his luck; he hadn't had a day like this in years. He nicked a like new Pentax 35mm camera, a Hitachi transistor radio with leather case, and a brand new pair of Ray Ban Aviator sunglasses. Things were going aces for Johnny Laskow until he spotted the pièce de résistance; some poor schmuck forgot his wallet on the seat of his car, the car's passenger side window was rolled down. He could see the hint of cash within the billfold, even if there wasn't a lot of cash, there probably was some credit cards, plastic gold, Things were looking good, this could be his El Dorado, all he had to do is not be too anxious, play it cool and be sure nobody was around.

He stood two cars away looking like he was waiting for someone; he would look at his watch then glance to the left and then the right. He was giving the performance of a lifetime; too bad thieves don't have awards like the Oscars for actors, because he was nailing it.

Johnny waited until he felt that the time was right, he walked over to the silver Buick Riviera, reached in the passenger's window, unlocked and opened the door, he leaned in grabbed the wallet, casually slid it into his back pocket and stood up, shut the door and was immediately surrounded by six uniformed police.

"Problem officer?"

"Is that your wallet sir?"

"Yes, I realized that it had slipped out of my pocket so I came back to retrieve it."

"May I see it sir."

"I can assure you it's my wallet officer."

"I'm sure it is sir, may I please have the wallet, Mr.?"

"Johnson. Johnny Johnson" Laskow tried to think of the most common name he could. Smith just seemed too phony. He pulled the wallet out of his pants pocket and handed the officer the wallet.

The police officer looked hard at Laskow and even before opening the wallet he said, "Do we know each other, Mr. Johnson? You look very familiar."

"No, I don't think so, officer. Although I get that a lot."

Officer Marten opened the wallet, took out the driver's license, then looked at Laskow, "Hmmm, the name on this license is a John Smith. Seems like you're under arrest Mr. Johnny Johnson."

"There must be some mistake, obviously I got my Riviera confused with this one."

"Okay, we'll play along, just where is your silver Buick Riviera, Mr. Johnson? And while we're looking for it we'll just place these handcuffs on you, if you don't mind. Did you forget these items too, Mr. Johnson? Funny, the radio has the name of Sally Rogers engraved on the back of it and the camera has a nametag taped on the bottom, and guess what, it isn't Johnny Johnson."

"Officer I can explain."

"Well, you can do all your explaining at the station, Mr. Johnson. Let's go."

As the police were walking Laskow to the squad car, Officer Masten handed the wallet to another policeman and said laughing, "Here's your wallet back Smiddy."

Once they were back at the 60th Precinct it didn't take too long for Officer Marten find out who Johnny Johnson really is, John Laskow three-time loser. As Laskow was getting fingerprinted and his mug shots taken, as luck would have Detective Sergeant Roscoe Brown was going to give an update to Captain O'Rourke, when he heard the officer fingerprinting Laskow say, "Man, that is one funky looking animal bite you got there man, maybe you should be checked out for rabies."

Roscoe stopped dead in his tracks; he walked in the fingerprinting area and said to the officer, "Jackie, I want a photograph of that bite right now. Let me see that."

He held Laskow's hand under a table lamp and there it was, the bite mark of a cat with a snaggle tooth. He just looked at the prisoner with such contempt, it took every fiber of his being not to drag this son of bitch out back into the alley and beat the living snot out of him, but he didn't, he just smiled knowing that this lowlife would soon be going up to Sing Sing for a date with the electric chair.

"Jackie, I also want what this man is wearing sent to the lab to check for fibers and cat hair, understand?"

"Right Detective Brown. Okay, strip, everything off, now."

"Hey, what am I going to put on, I can't be standing here naked as a jaybird."

"Oh, you're going to be given brand new state issue khaki's. You'll be very stylish when you're waiting to die at Sing." Roscoe smirked.

"For what stealing a lousy camera and radio!"

"No, for robbing, raping and bludgeoning to death a seventy-eight-year-old woman. Book him for murder. You know Laskow, you might have gotten away with murder Laskow, if only you left the cat alone."

"You can't prove nothing with a damn cat!"

"Au contraire, my friend. You'll see."

"What does that mean?"

"Meow."

The next morning Roscoe had Betty bring the cat down to the crime lab, so they could get an impression of Lucifer's unique bite pattern and compare it to the bite mark on Johnny Laskow. They also took some fur samples and see if they were a match for cat hairs found on Laskow's clothes.

Overnight, Detective's Brown and Walsh went to the suspect's place of residence with a search warrant and found tools, jewelry, wallets, purses, assorted stolen items and one lead pipe with a rubber grip that had what appeared to be blood on it.

Later that day they got the report from the coroner and the lab, Roscoe, and Walsh took a drive to Rikers Island to confront Johnny Laskow to inform him that the D.A. was charging him with capital murder and seeking the death penalty.

When Laskow arrived at the interrogation room, he had several cuts and bruises on his face, he had a black eye and a split lip, when Roscoe saw that he was injured he asked the guard, "What the hell happened to this prisoner?"

"Inmates don't like people who rape children and old lady's."

Walsh looked at Laskow, "Is that what happened, other inmates did this to you?"

Laskow just nodded affirmatively.

"Well, I want him to be held in isolation, he should and will be punished, but not by a bunch of vigilantes," Roscoe told the guard. As much as he wanted Laskow to suffer for killing Mrs. Stieferman, he didn't deserve this.

"You'll have to take that up with the warden."

Walsh told Roscoe that he'd take care of seeing that Laskow would be put in protective custody, "I'll be back in a few." He said and left with the guard.

"You got to believe me, I didn't kill anyone."

"Mr. Laskow you're lying, your only hope of beating the electric chair is a truthful confession.

"Look we got a positive match on the cat bite, your clothes had cat fur on it, the same fur that Mrs. Stieferman's cat has, we have the testimony of three pawn shop owners who have positively identified you as the man who hocked the victims jewelry and we have the murder weapon found in your apartment with the victim's blood on it and to top it all off, your blood was found at the scene. All in all, not a good day for you Mr. Laskow."

Johnny knew it was all over; he sat there staring at the hand where that stupid cat had bitten him and said more to himself than to the Detective sitting across from him, "Never did like cats, they're the Devil in disguise. Yeah, I killed her. What do you want to know?"

!! 🔔†☆⚓🐾💀❄⚡!!

"Jimmy, I'm so glad that you could come." Betty said as she answered the knock at the door.

"Thank you for inviting me for dinner, these are for you." He said as he handed her a bouquet of wildflowers.

"They're beautiful, thank you. Come in, come in."

"Hey Jimmy, care for something to drink? Beer, wine, pop?" Roscoe asked.

"I'll have whatever you're having."

"Beer it is." He said as he handed him an ice-cold Rheingold.

"Thanks."

"So, what's the buzz?"

"Well Laskow, got 99 years and a day, so there's no chance of parole ever, but at least he beat the devil."

"And speaking of the devil." Lucifer walks into the living room and rubs up against Walsh's leg.

"Well, I love this little devil." Betty confesses.

Roscoe smiles and says, "I guess that makes us a couple of Devil worshipers."

"You know Roscoe, you were pretty lucky on Laskow."

"Well Jimmy, I'd rather be lucky, than good."

The Case of 3 Wives Dead

"And do you, Roger Rogers take Sally Clark to be your wedded wife, to have and to hold, from this day forward, for better, for worse, for richer, for poorer, in sickness and in health, to love and to cherish, till death do us part, according to God's holy ordinance; and thereto do you pledge your faith yourself to her?"

It was a beautiful wedding; everyone could see how much these two crazy kids were in love. Everyone except the bride's father, who thought that his new son-in-law was a real low-life weasel. The bum didn't have a steady job, they were going to live in his basement and pay no rent until Roger got a job, yeah right!

Roger and Sally had been only known each other a short time; according to Roger, he knew she was the one the moment he set eyes on her standing in line at the New York Free Clinic. Sally was there for a pregnancy test, and Roger to see if he contracted VD.

Sally had been attending Kingsborough Community College, better known as Coney Island City College, the home of the "Fighting Whitefish." She's was taking classes in Tourism and Hospitality, hoping to get a job at one of the big hotels in Manhattan someday.

Roger hadn't set the bar that high for himself, his main interest in life was doing nothing, he spent a lot of time in the gym working out, and he would occasionally try a little thievery, or selling assorted drugs, like weed, zoomers, blow, mixed jive, China White, toe-tag dope, or even some of that new shit, LSD. He had tried some and it really blew his mind.

He also had a passion for sex; he found that having just one wife didn't satisfy his needs. That's why he had three; Hell, old Solomon in the Bible had 700 wives and 300 concubines. Roger found that 2 wives just didn't cut it and four was crazy too many, but three wives were perfect. He calls them his Holy Trinity.

There was his first wife Daisy, Daisy was almost ten years older, she worked in Manhattan as a paralegal for a large Wall Street firm. She liked the fact that she had a younger lover, He looked like James Dean, he had a terrific body, he was good looking and best of all he had a voracious sexual appetite, if she was in the mood he could go three or four times a night and would want more, she would often say, "Listen baby, momma's got to get some sleep, remember I got to go to work. Now go to sleep."

Suzie was wife number two, she worked at his gym, was his age, twenty-five and had a rock hard body. Naked they looked like Ken and Barbie dolls, except they had genitals. They often made love after hours using the gym's fitness equipment, sauna room, steam room, Jacuzzi and the gymnastic gear. While Suzie likes to kink it up, she would only want sex two or three times a week, not enough for Roger.

Wife number three was five years younger than Roger, she was sexually inexperienced and he really liked that about her, he could mold her into the sexual partner of his desire. Three wives and each brought something unique to the party, plus they all worked, so they could support him. He told them that he was a private investigator, which gave him the excuse why he had to be away from each of them for days at a time. And since most of his work involved the government, it was all pretty much hush hush. He would say that his work was the sort of thing that if he told you, he'd have to kill you. They either believed him or else they thought the sex was so great they didn't care.

Things were going just how Roger had envisioned them, he was living three lives with three wives, and lives were good until he got arrested for selling marijuana to an undercover narc on the boardwalk.

Since Roger didn't have an attorney, he was appointed a public defender, David Rosenbaum Esquire, a recent graduate of New York Law School. David was too new to have earned the moniker of being considered a 'dump truck' lawyer.

Some public defenders get saddled as being 'dump trucks,' lawyers because defendant's belief that defenders aren't interested in giving a vigorous defense, but rather seek only to 'dump' them as quickly as possible. But not David Rosenbaum Esquire, this was his first case out of college and he saw it as an opportunity to shine, to show the world what a great attorney he is, even though he graduated last in his class, his theory was, somebody has to last.

"Mr. Rogers, my name is David Rosenbaum, I've been appointed as your attorney. I see here that you've been charged with possession of a controlled substance and drug trafficking."

"Yeah, this bogus, man."

"So, you didn't try and sell the marijuana to the police officer?"

"No, I did. But don't they have to identify themselves as cops?"

"No, they don't Mr. Rogers."

"That doesn't seem fair. Hey, he came up to me and asked if I was holding, isn't that entrapment?"

"No, it isn't. Did you do or say anything that would lead the officer to believe that you had drugs or that you were selling drugs?"

"Well, I was smoking a joint at the time."

"So, you were standing out on the street smoking marijuana when a stranger approaches you and asks if you had any drugs for sale, is that correct?"

"Yeah."

"And then what did you say after he asked you if you had any drugs for sale?"

"I said you bet, how much do you want. He said he wanted a kilo, and I said are you nuts, I don't have anything like that, but I can sell you a nickel bag. And that's when he told me he was a cop and I was under arrest. It sure seems like entrapment to me."

"Well, it's not. Now Mr. Rogers, we're going to plead not guilty. Do you have any prior arrests or convictions, Mr. Rogers?"

"Nope."

"Well that's good, now let me try and get bail for you, who should I call."

Roger gave Rosenbaum the phone numbers of all three wives, he figured between the three of them they could arrange for his bail.

"Are these women all related to you, Mr. Rogers?"

"Yeah, they're my wives."

"Your wives, plural?"

"No, triple."

"You have three wives? Mr. Rogers, don't you know that's against the law? That's bigamy."

"Can't be against the law, King Solomon had 700 wives. I only got three."

"Do these women know about the other wives?"

"No."

"Well, if the police find out that you have three wives, you could get up to five years in prison plus a $10,000 dollar fine. It's considered a class E felony."

"So, here just call Daisy, she'll come down and bail me out. You won't tell anybody will you Mr. Rosenbaum?"

"No, but I recommend you resolve this issue before too long."

"Oh yes sir, I surely will."

!! 🕯️🔫💀☠️⚡!!

"Roger, what were you thinking? You've put me in a real bind with my law firm; they're not going to be too thrilled that my husband has been arrested for drug trafficking and possession."

"Do they have to find out?"

"I'm sure they will eventually, then I'm screwed. You really fucked up royally!"

"Calm down, babe."

"Calm down! You've basically ruined my career, how could you be so stupid!"

The more she got upset, the more he didn't, and that was really starting to annoy her, he didn't seem to care that his foolish actions had such a devastating impact on her career.

Then she totally lost it when he lit up a joint and offered it to her, "Here Daisy, take a couple deep drags on this. It will help you chill out."

She knocked it out of his hand and slapped him hard across the face and shouted, "You asshole, I hate you!"

Stunned, Roger stood motionless for a moment, and then something in his head just snapped, the next thing he remembered was his hands around her neck, squeezing as hard as he could. She was collapsing down towards the ground and he just followed her down continuing to squeeze. Her face was contorted in pain; she had her hands on his hands trying desperately to loosen his grip, but to no avail. Her face was turning blue as her eyes were starting to roll up into the back of her head, then she became limp, motionless, dead.

He stood up, straddling her lifeless body looking down at her lying with a surreal and eerie expression on her face, her eyes weren't open and yet they weren't closed and yet they seemed to be looking at him no matter where he stood in the room.

He went into the kitchen and fixed himself a scotch and water, then walked back out into the living room, sat down on the couch and tried to think. He thought it was a bit ironic that his wife lay dead in the 'living' room', weird. He finished his drink and was going to try and make it look like someone else did this but knew that it would a waste of time. So, he decided to go home to wife number two.

Suzie stood in the bedroom doorway wearing pink see-through baby doll pajamas.

"Roger, hi baby, what a pleasant surprise, I wasn't expecting you for a couple more days." Suzie said.

"I got done early, so I could get back to you."

"Aw, that's so sweet. Come on baby let's go to bed."

!! 👤†✿⁂☠✳🔑 !!

Detective's Brown and Walsh got the call at four in the morning that there had been a domestic disturbance at 3049 Brighton 3rd Street, Brighton Beach some neighbors called in a complaint of shouting and screaming. When the uniforms got there they could see thru the window curtains what looked to be a body of a woman lying on the floor.

Officer Hancock, a six foot six African American, tipping the scales at a mere 280 pounds of solid muscle popped the front door open like it was unlocked.

When they entered they found a woman on the living room floor that appeared to have been strangled. That's when dispatch called Brown and Walsh, who arrived at the same time as the coroner.

"Whatda we got, Hancock?" Roscoe asked.

"Daisy Rogers looks to be in her mid-thirties, Caucasian, and looks she was strangled, she is wearing a wedding ring. There are signs of a struggle, but no forced entry and it doesn't appear to be anything missing and the husband is nowhere to be found. I checked, and this guy Roger Rogers was just arrested earlier this evening on a couple drug charges and she's the one who bailed him out."

"Roger Rogers? What kind of parents would name their kid Roger Rogers?" Walsh asked.

"Parents, that stutter?" Roscoe quipped.

"Good one."

"Okay, while the ME is doing his thing, let's snoop around."

They each took separate rooms, Walsh took the living room and kitchen and Roscoe started in the bedroom and bath. Looking around the bedroom Roscoe found that in the closet there were both Daisy's and her husband's clothes, her clothes were that of a professional while his primary jeans and tee shirts. It was true what Betty says, when it comes to clothes, there's only room for one peacock in a relationship and she was definitely the peacock.

There were several framed photographs on one of the dressers of the victim and her husband, they were a nice looking couple, Roscoe had seen this sort of thing happen all the time, one of them does something stupid like getting picked up for drugs and the whole thing goes into the crapper.

On her nightstand, ironically was a hardback copy of Truman Capote's In Cold Blood, on his nightstand was a stack of Mad Magazines. The Detective figured out what this relationship was built on, she was the serious one bringing in the paycheck and he was a man-child, who after finding several sex toys in both of their bed stands was more her lover than her husband.

So, he gets his self-arrested and she blows up, she sees that he's putting her career in jeopardy and maybe the sex isn't worth all the aggravation and grief. She loses it, they fight, she dies, and he runs. Now, it's just a matter of time till they catch him.

"The ME said definitely strangulation, he'll get us the report late afternoon. You find anything?" Walsh asks coming in from the living room.

"Yeah, the same old story, she's the adult and he's the petulant child. Let's go back to the station and send out an APB and description to find this Roger Rogers."

"Roger Rogers, with a name like that this poor slob was destined to be a nut job."

"Well, like Shakespeare said, "What's in a name?"

‼️💣🕯️✳️🔅☠️✳️⚡‼️

"Hey, wake up sleepy head." Suzie said standing by Roger's side of the bed holding two cups of coffee. She held out one for him.

"Here ya go."

"What time is it?" He asked dazed, after the events of last night he was still a bit befuddled and confused. Had he really strangled Daisy or was it all just a bad dream?

"It's eight-thirty and I got to get going, the gym opens at nine."

He took her hand and pulled her down to the bed and whispered, "Why don't you call in sick?"

She kissed him on the cheek, jumped up and finished her coffee. On the way out of the bedroom she laughed and said, "You're terrible, now get up and walk me to work, you bum."

He slipped on his Levis button fly jeans, didn't bothered with any underwear, underwear was for the uptight corporate types, threw on a ragged old sweatshirt and a pair of ratty old Converse high-top sneakers, the uniform of the anti-establishment movement.

They walked hand in hand down Bath Avenue to the corner of 20th Avenue where she worked, Jim's Gym. The gym had been a part of Bath Beach for over thirty years; it was originally a gym for boxers, but unlike other gyms in New York Jim's Gym never produced a contender, so it slowly began to move into the modern age of gyms, offering not only dead weights but also some workout machines. Soon even a couple of women came into workout.

When they reached the doorway she asked, "You wanna come and work out, you look a mess."

"Maybe a little later, I got a couple things I got to do."

"Okay, I love you."

"Love you too."

After he left her, he worked his way back to Daisy's, taking obscure streets in hopes that he wouldn't be recognized should he see a cop. He reached his block going undetected and saw a police car outside the house and a uniformed police officer standing on the stoop. Roger walked past the house on the other side of the street being careful not to look at the cop. He quickly turned the corner and made his way back to Suzie's place, where he spent the rest of the day expecting the police to bust thru the front door any minute or maybe lob some tear gas in thru window.

To take his mind off the cops, he turned on Suzie's new Zenith Console color television. Flipping thru the three channels, he settled on the Price is Right; it was just what he needed, something mindless. Roger sat there on the couch watching television for over six hours until the news came on. He just knew that Daisy's death was going to be a lead story, and it was.

"And in Brighton Beach last night, police responded to a 911 domestic quarrel call only to discover the murder of this woman, Daisy Rogers, the police are asking if anyone knows the whereabouts of her husband Roger Rogers in connection with the murder his wife. At this time he is only a person of interest. If you have any information please call the tips hotline. Also in the news...."

"Damn, that can't be good."

‼ 👻🕇☆🔩💀🏵⚡‼

Roscoe and Walsh ran Roger Rogers name thru their database, except for last night's arrest he hadn't been in any sort of trouble, not even a parking ticket. What would drive a seemingly nice guy to commit murder, maybe the thought of possible prison time freaked him out or maybe the wife was so apoplectic and hysterical that she set him off down a road where he ended up choking her to death.

Right now he was their only suspect, they needed to speak to him, if for no other reason than to eliminate him as a suspect.

Walsh came into Roscoe's office, "Well I checked with the arresting officer, he said that since Rogers was only trying to sell him a nickel bag, he'd probably would have gotten off with probation."

"So, something had to set him off, he must have an attorney, let's see if we can get him down here."

"Okay, I'll give him a call."

Three hours later, David Rosenbaum Esquire was waiting downstairs at the Desk Sergeant.

"Could you send him up to my office Jerry, thanks."

Walsh was sitting across from Brown when David Rosenbaum attorney for Roger Rogers knock on the doorsill,

'Detective Brown, I'm David Rosenbaum, Mr. Rogers public defender, how can I be of service?"

"Come in and have a seat Mr. Rosenbaum, I want to thank you for coming down."

Roger's attorney sat next to Detective Walsh across from Roscoe.

"Mr. Rosenbaum, do you know why I asked to see you?"

"I do not. Unless it's about the drug charges."

"At this point that is the least of possible problems facing Mr. Rogers. Last night after his wife bailed him out of jail and later on this morning, she was found strangled in her home. And we don't seem able to find him. At this time we need to speak with him, he's not a suspect but a person of interest. Would you happen to know where he might be?"

"I'm afraid I don't, Detective." The rookie attorney said, but then he let slip a bombshell.

Not thinking, Rosenbaum asked, "Which wife was killed?"

The moment it came out of his mouth he knew he screwed up big time, and he quickly tried to walk it back. But as they say, you can't unring a bell.

"Ah, I mean where was she killed?"

Roscoe and Walsh both perked up, it was as if they snapped to attention. They said the same thing at the exact same time in unison, "How many does he have?"

"Oh, I don't know what you're talking about. My, my look at the time, I really must be going. Sorry I couldn't be any help. Goodbye Detectives." And with that, he was gone like a shot from a cannon.

"Walsh, let's find out just how many wives our Mr. Rogers has."

80

Suzie found Roger sitting in the dark apartment watching The Beverly Hillbillies on television.

"Whatca doing babe? How come you didn't come down to the gym?"

"Just not in the mood."

"What's the matter, are you okay?"

Roger wasn't okay, an hour earlier a couple of plainclothes knocked on the door, he saw them thru the blinds. He pretended that no one was home and they left, but he knew they'll be back. Roger wondered how they know he's got another wife, must be that damn lawyer of his. Now it won't be long until Suzie knows.

"Yeah, I'm better now that you're home, why don't we go take a nap, if you know what I mean and I think you do. After let's order in a pizza, whadda say?"

She started to get undressed as she walked towards the bedroom; by the time she got to the bed, she was completely naked. She laid down and watched as Roger get undressed, he kneeled down next to her an slowly turned her over.

"Mmmm, yeah it's been a long time since we did it from behind." She purred.

As he was rocking back and forth, in and out he was sliding his hands up and down her back, then when she arched her back upward Roger grabbed her by the throat and began to squeeze. At first, she thought he was trying something new and it felt exciting, but then he started squeezing harder and she couldn't breathe, the harder he pushed himself inside her the tighter his grip became until she was struggling for her life. The more she struggled the more he became excited and the harder he choked until she collapsed forward flat on the bed.

Roger left her dead nude body lying on the bed while he showered and shaved. With two of the three wives dead at least they couldn't charge him with bigamy.

81

He sat at the foot of the bed naked and wet talking out loud to himself, "I bet King Salomon never had this problem. I wonder what Salomon would do? I bet if he couldn't have all his wives, then he wouldn't want any. It's all or nothing for me and old Salomon."

He got dressed, turned off the television and left the front door unlocked and slightly ajar, so when the cops came back again, they'd find her the way he displayed her, spread eagle on the bed.

It was a little after 10 p.m. when he peered out the backdoor, making sure there weren't any police outside waiting for him. He walked down the alley close to the fences so he would be hard to see. By eleven he got to the Clark's house, it looked like the in-laws were fast asleep.

His and Sally's apartment was down in the basement; he went inside and found his bride sleeping. Not wanting to alarm her he undressed and made enough noise to bring her out of her sleep.

She opened her eyes, smiled and said, "Hey Roger, oh how I've missed you, come and make love to me, baby."

Never one to disappoint the ladies, Roger always aimed to please and this time was no exception. Later they lay side by side fast asleep until seven in the morning when they could hear the footsteps of her family above.

"Hey baby, do you have any classes today?"

"Just a poli sci class at one."

"Skip it, let's spend the whole day in bed together."

"Wish I could, but today's my finals."

Roger disappointed, threw off the blanket and got up.

"Where are you going?"

"Got to take a leak."

As he stood at the toilet urinating, he looked at his self in the medicine cabinet and thought, why are all my wives treating me like crap, all I asked was for her to spend the day with me, her husband. Salomon wouldn't stand for any of his wives disrespecting him or disobeying him.

When he returned, he climbed in bed. She was turned with her back to him, he gently grabbed her a turned her over like he did Suzie, this time be placed a couple pillows under her stomach so her ass would still be up when she was dead. He proceeded to enter her from behind; he started rubbing her back as his body moved forward and backward until she too arched her back in such a way that he could easily clutch her neck.

Sally was a lot more petite than Suzie, so it was over quicker. With Sally, he covered her with the blanket so if her parents found her she would look like she was asleep. Once he had done that, he left. He didn't have a plan, he never had a plan, he always acted spontaneously.

He always thought of himself a wild and crazy guy. Maybe he'd go out west, California or Nevada someplace like that where he could get lost, but he didn't have a car. Things like that never stopped him before. After a while when things cooled down he could get married again. Then he remembered Utah might be just the place to go, he heard they let you have lots of wives there. He'd even be okay with wearing the special underwear if he could have lots of wives.

!! ☠†☼⚒☠✴⚡ !!

Roscoe and Walsh returned to Suzie Rogers' apartment, when they got to the front door they noticed that it was slightly opened. They both drew their revolvers and carefully entered the dark foyer; Jim reached over to the wall and flipped the light switch on.

Jim shouted, "Police! Anybody here?"

Roscoe gestured that they both move towards the bedroom. Guns drawn, they carefully moved down the hall, the bedroom door was closed, again Jim announced their presence, "Police!"

Standing on either side of the doorway, Roscoe turned the doorknob and let the door swing open, they waited a beat then they both entered to see Suzie Rogers lying spread eagle totally naked on the bed. Her head was tilted slightly back and her eyes were gazing up to the ceiling.

"This is one crazy, mother." Walsh declared.

"Let's get the ME down here now, we got to catch this freak and fast. How many more marriages with the name Rogers are there?"

"According to the city, there's four more."

"Well, let's send out the uniforms to check on the others."

Walsh and Roscoe searched the entire house and found several pictures of Roger and Suzie; it was the same Roger that had been married to Daisy. So, they confirmed that they are looking for the same guy.

Walsh let the coroner into the apartment along with the crime lab folks. Roscoe found her gym employee identification badge in her purse.

"Hey Walsh, let's go and talk to the folks at this gym." He said holding up her ID.

The concept of Jim's Gym may have been to modernize it by adding workout machines and a new coat of paint, but the whole place smelled like a basket full of old used jock straps.

They stood at the reception desk for a couple of minutes waiting for this knuckle dragger in a wife beater tee shirt to stop hitting on this little red-headed chirpy, flexing his muscles and striking poses trying to impress her.

"Hey, muscles! Get over here."

The gym rat hunkered over carrying a tough guy attitude, "Yeah, what do ya want?"

Roscoe held up his badge, "I want to talk to the owner."

"What for, cop?"

"Listen, tough guy, you want to crack wise with me? I'll throw your ass in a jail cell for obstruction of justice so fast it will make your head spin. Take you down to Rikers; you'll end up as somebody's old lady in no time. Am I right Walsh?"

"Yeah, they'll be fighting over you sweetheart."

"Sorry, I didn't mean nothing by it. I'll go get Louie."

The big lummox ran up the stairs and within seconds a short, stocky, balding man came toddling down the stairs wearing a fighter's training shirt with the name Jim stitched over the left pocket.

"Can I help you officer?"

"You Jim?"

"No, I'm Louie Saddler, the owner. Jim's been dead over twenty years now. It gets too complicated going around explaining about Jim, so to keep it simple, I'm Jim. Besides, it costs too much money to change the name to Louie's Gym and Jim's Gym has a nice ring to it, don't ya think?"

"Sure. Louie, I'm Detective Sergeant Brown and this is Detective Walsh when was the last time you saw Suzie Rogers?"

"About five o'clock this afternoon. Why, what did that creep of a husband do?"

"What do you mean? Has he caused trouble around here?

"Yeah, that no good bum doesn't work, takes advantage of that sweet kid, always bumming money off her. He comes in here an works out sometimes, don't pay for nothing, but because I like Suzie I let him get away with it. Last week I threw him out for good, the little punk was hanging out trying to sell dope. I told him if he came around again I'd break his legs. So, I haven't seen the weasel since then."

"Do you or anyone here might know any of his friends?"

"Friends? That jerk didn't have any friends. Can you tell me if Suzie's okay?"

"I'm afraid not, she was found murdered this afternoon."

The fireplug of a man started to cry like a baby, "She worked here for over five years, I loved that girl like a daughter. I can't believe she's gone."

"Do you know if she had a family?"

"I think her father passed away and her mother lives somewhere in Florida."

Walsh put his hand on the man's shoulder and said, "I'm so sorry Louie. If you see Rogers, here are our cards, please call us right away."

"I just pray to God that I do see that little shit."

"You call us, Louie. Don't do anything foolish understand." Walsh's tone went from consolatory to authoritative, driving his point home.

Roscoe and Walsh decided to head back to the station and see if they heard anything from the unis.

Roger came to a climax even though Sally was dead, he then went and took a shower, came back to where Sally's lifeless body was lying face down in the mattress and her backside raised up with pillows under her stomach. The way she was positioned, reminded him of when Suzie did her yoga workout, the position she called the extended puppy pose.

He removed the pillows from under her and laid her flat in the bed on her back and covered with the blanket, finally he closed her eyes. She looked so restful, so peaceful, so dead.

Roger got dressed, looked at the clock on the bed stand, 4 a.m., time to go to West. He figured he'd steal cars and take a leisurely drive cross-country, but he needed some protection.

Mr. Lee Clark was a World War 2 veteran, a sergeant in Patton's Third Army, fought in the Battle of the Bulge, was wounded, won the Purple Heart, and 2 Bronze Stars. As a souvenir from "The Big One", Lee brought home a German Luger pistol that he kept in the den in a lower drawer of his desk upstairs.

Roger climbed the creaky stairs up from the basement, opened the door the led into the kitchen and found Armageddon, the family's 150-pound German shepherd sitting with his lips pulled back exposing teeth take could rip his throat out and a low guttural growl emanating deep within his gullet.

"Nice boy, good boy." Roger whispered as he slowly tiptoed from the kitchen to the den with Armageddon following right behind him. He opened the bottom drawer, found the Luger, a box of shells and walked back to the basement door, all the while being literally dogged all the way. He managed to retrieve the gun and get back into the basement without being eaten alive by that killer dog.

Out on the streets, it was still dark, but the sun was starting to lighten the eastern sky. The Clarks live in a very suburban neighborhood in Manhattan Beach at 31 Dover Street, a couple blocks from the main drag, Shore Drive where he turned right and crossed over the Ocean Avenue Pedestrian Bridge into Sheepshead Bay.

He walked over three hours until he reached Sheepshead Bay Yacht Club parking lot where he was hoping to steal a car, unfortunately, they were all locked, except for a red MGB roadster, it even had the key in the ignition.

Vroom! How lucky he thought, things were finally breaking his way. That is until he tried to put the car in drive, but there was no drive, the MGB has a manual transmission not an automatic one and poor old Roger never learned to drive a stick shift. He sat there lurching and jerking and stalling every five feet, it would take him years just to get over to New Jersey at this rate.

By now people were starting to emerge from their homes heading to work, go shopping or because it was such a nice day get out and walk along the bay walk.

A man wearing one of those funny English tweed-driving caps came running towards the MGB, shouting, "Stop thief! Stop that man!" Roger abandoned the car and started running along the bay walk until he thought it better to get off the busy Emmons Avenue, so he ran left up Ford Street for half a block.

The MGB owner spotted a patrol car cruising in the opposite direction, he flagged him down and gave the police officers a description of the car thief and which way he was running. The driver turned the squad car around and flipped the switch for the flashing lights and siren, while the other police officer called in that they were in pursuit of a possible car thief.

As Roger was running, he was wildly looking for a place to hide, that's when he saw his opportunity. A small brick duplex on his left, a woman was saying goodbye to her husband heading off to work, everything looked to Roger like it was meant to be, the little iron fence gate was open, the couple were standing in the open doorway, so he sprinted thru the iron gate and by the time he cleared the three porch steps he had the Luger out and pointing it at the young couple.

"Get in the house, now!" Roger shouted as the police car stopped in front of 2826 Ford Street. The driver pulled his revolver and stood behind a large oak tree by the curb. The other officer called in to dispatch that they now have a hostage crisis.

The couple, Richard and Debbie Steinberg did as they were told. Roger had Tony sit on the couch in the living room while he took Debbie by the arm and went from room to room making sure all the windows and doors were locked. He told Tony that if got off the couch or he tried anything he would shoot his wife.

Within minutes the whole neighborhood was crawling with police, the little house was completely surrounded and under siege. With all the blinds drawn and windows closed, the police outside waited for the hostage negotiators to arrive.

Roger cracked the front door and shouted out, "Nobody try anything, I've got two hostages and I'll kill them both if I have to, so stay away."

!! ●†☼⚘☠☀⚡!!

Police Officer Raymond Johnson rang the doorbell at 7:30 a.m. Lee Clark answered the door already dressed for work.

"Mr. Rogers?" Officer Johnson asked.

"No, I'm Lee Clark, Rogers is married to my daughter, they live in the apartment in the basement. Can I help you?"

"Actually, I need to speak to either if I may."

"Please come in, don't mind the dog, he's a pussycat. Armageddon go lay down." The dog did as he was told.

"He's beautiful, but he sure doesn't look like a pussycat."

The two men made their way to the basement door in the kitchen, Mr. Clark knocked, "Sally."

Nothing. He knocked and called out several times, he finally unlocked the door and started down the staircase,

"Sally, its dad. There's a police officer that needs to speak to you, Sally."

They stood in the small living room, Mr. Clark said, "Excuse me officer, let me look in the bedroom."

Johnson heard Mr. Clark try and wake his daughter. Officer Johnson ran into the bedroom when he heard Mr. Clark scream out, "Sally! God no, Sally!"

Johnson took over; he separated Mr. Clark from cradling her daughter's body. "Mr. Clark you must let go you might be contaminating the crime scene. Please, Mr. Clark put her down."

Lee Clark placed his daughter's head back on to the pillow ever so gently and gave her a kiss on her forehead, then went upstairs crying to tell his wife. Officer Johnson called into the station, "This is Johnson, we have a 187 at 2841 West 22nd Street, please alert Detective Brown and Walsh, also get the coroner down here too. Over."

Officer Johnson went upstairs to wait for everyone outside, as he was reached the kitchen he heard the wailing and sobbing of Mrs. Clark. He locked the door and went outside. Thirty minutes later Brown and Walsh pulled up to the Clark's house to find Officer Johnson waiting for them by the front door.

"Hey Ray, what do we have?"

"I am thinking it's strangulation, there are ligature marks on her neck. It looks like he killed her from behind. When we found her she was in bed and covered up as if she was asleep."

Downstairs next to her bed stand was a wedding photo of the happy couple, she looked so young an innocent, so angelic, he looked rather dashing in his tuxedo. How were the family to know he would turn out to be a cold-blooded killer and right in their own home?

The coroner showed up and affirmed it was indeed strangulation, just like the others. The two Detectives let the

ME and crime lab do their thing, while they would have the unpleasant task of talking to the parents.

"Mr. and Mrs. Clark, we're so sorry for your loss. I know it hard right now, but we need to ask you a few questions. Would that be alright?" Roscoe asked.

"Sure." Lee Clark said as he held his wife in his close in his arms, her face was buried in his chest silently sobbing.

"What can you tell us about Roger Rogers?"

"I was against this marriage from the get-go, there was something about him that just wasn't right. He said he worked for several detective agencies, but he never would say which ones. He'd be gone for days, sometimes weeks, telling Sally that he was on a case. Case my ass. He's a lousy punk and I pray to God you catch or better yet kill the bastard."

Officer Johnson entered the living room, "Sorry to interrupt Detective but I think we may found the suspect."

"Where?"

"Someone fitting Rogers description has taken a couple of hostages over in Sheepshead Bay, he says he's armed and threatens to kill them if the police try anything. The hostage negotiators are on their way."

Roscoe turned to Mr. Clark, "Do you have any weapons in the house, Mr. Clark?"

"I have a German Luger I brought back from the war. It should be in the bottom drawer in the den."

Walsh said, "I'll go check."

Minutes later he came back, "No gun."

"That little hooligan." Clark said to himself.

"Mr. Clark, Officer Johnson will remain here until we return. You folks stay here and don't go near the basement; we'll be back as soon as we can.

"Ray, take charge of the scene."

"Yes sir."

"Come on Jim, let's go."

!! ☙†☆�.☠❈☠❡!!

Lieutenant Collins of the Hostage Negotiation Division got to the scene and immediately took command. He had all the officer's stay in position, but out of sight, he had the electricity and the water shut off, then he did nothing for two hours while he got the phone number of the residence.

It was almost noon before he called.

"Hello?"

"Who am I speaking with, please?"

"Who are you?"

"This is Lieutenant Collins."

"Are you in charge?"

"Yes."

"And you are?"

"Roger."

"Talk to me, Roger."

"I want all you cops to leave, I want a car with automatic transmission, a quarter of a million dollars in small denominations and I want a two-hour head start and then I'll let these people go."

"I want to fuck Audrey Hepburn, but that ain't gonna happen, now Roger I'm afraid we just can't go away, you know that. What I can do is promise that if you give yourself up you'll be treated with respect and courtesy."

"Listen, I got two hostages in here and if I don't get what I want, I'm gonna start kill people."

"How many people you have hostage, Roger?"

"Two."

"Let me hear them and so I know that they're not injured."

Roger handed the phone to the young woman sitting on the couch. "Say something!"

"Hello?"

"Hello, who is this?"

"I'm Debbie Steinberg and my husband is Richard."

"Debbie are you alright?"

"Yes we're fine, just scared."

"Don't worry Debbie, everything is going to be fine, just stay calm. Let me speak to Roger."

"He wants to speak to you." Debbie said as she handed the phone to the man holding gun at her.

"So, now what?" Roger asked.

"So, now we negotiate. How about, I give you the money, but you have to let the girl go."

"No way!"

"Look, Roger, we got what you want and you got what we want. So, let's start trading, it's only fair, right?"

"Let's see the money, and no funny stuff."

"The money will be here within the hour, so just sit tight and be cool. You getting hungry, want I should get you a pizza?"

"Yeah, a pizza would be nice."

"Pepperoni?"

"With mushrooms, green peppers, and pineapple."

"Okay, it's on the way. Stay near the phone, I'll call when it gets here."

"Yeah, okay."

Collins hung up the phone, waved over a uniformed and said, "Get this jamoke a pepperoni pizza with pineapple."

"Pineapple? Who the fuck eats pizza with pineapple?"

"Just order the damn thing."

"From anywhere in particular?" the officer asked.

Lieutenant Collins gave the officer a look of, are you serious and said, "Just get a freaking pizza!."

As the officer was walking away Collins quipped, "Anywhere in particular."

Detectives Brown and Walsh arrived and found Collins arranging for the money to be delivered when he got off the phone with Bank of America, Brown inquired, "How's it going, Bobby?"

"We're dealing with a real mental midget here. But I'm thinking if all goes well, it should be over soon. I've got snipers lined up and a couple tricks up my sleeve. I understand this is your wife killer."

"Wives. He was married to three women and has killed all three. So fyi, he might want to go out in a blaze of glory."

"Thanks, Roscoe, I'll keep that in mind."

A few minutes later an armored car pulled up as did the officer with the pizza. Collins called the house and Roger answered it in the first ring.

"Hello."

"Roger, this is Lieutenant Collins, I have your pizza and the money. Now, I'm going to bring you the money and pizza, I'll be unarmed. When I get to the door I'll place the money and pizza inside the door and you have Debbie ready to leave with me. Understand?"

"How do I know that's real money and not just paper?"

"I'll have the bag unzipped so you can see it, okay?"

"Okay, but no funny stuff."

"No funny stuff."

Collins gave the pizza officer his weapon, took the pizza and bag of money and headed towards the front door. He had already given the order that if any of the snipers had a clear shot, to go for it.

As he approached the door, he did a slow turn around to show that he wasn't carrying a piece. The front door cracked open as Collins reached the top stair, he placed the bag down and unzipped it to show stacks and stacks of twenty-dollar bills.

"Can you see the money, Roger?"

"Yeah."

"Okay, now I'm going to place the money and the pizza inside, is Debbie there?"

"Yes, I'm here."

"Okay, Roger open the door so I can place everything inside."

As Roger opened the door, Lieutenant Collins observed that Roger was standing behind the door, the husband was sitting on the couch in the living room and Debbie was to his left. Before he set the money into the foyer he feigned a sneeze and brought up his right arm, which signaled the snipers to take the shot at the front door once Collins had grabbed Debbie out of the line of fire.

As soon as Collins placed the bag of money and pizza inside the house, he grabbed Debbie by the arm pulling her out the door onto the lawn. He could hear the fire coming from the sniper's rifles and sensed the bullets whizzing by them while they were still in midair, then within seconds officers busted in thru the front door and the back door as well.

Roger had been shot six times, amazingly none of the wounds was life-threatening. The paramedics were there on site and addressed his injuries while they rushed him to Brooklyn Community Hospital, ten minutes away. Detective's Brown and Walsh were right behind them.

As the paramedics were loading Rogers into the ambulance, Brown, and Walsh passed by Collins, who was eating a piece of pepperoni pizza.

"You guys want a slice?"

"Pizza with pineapple, Bobby?"

"Fuck you guys."

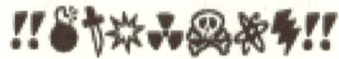

Roger Rogers lie handcuffed to a bed in Brooklyn Community Hospital with a tube snaked down his nose, a couple IV tubes in his arms, and a colostomy bag attached to his left groin. Roger had six bullet wounds, four passed right through him, one took off three fingers of his right hand and the other removed a chunk of his skull the size of a tennis ball.

"Mr. Rogers, I'm Detective Brown and this is my partner, Detective Walsh. How are you feeling? Because you look like shit."

Rogers didn't say anything he just stared, he was coming out of the anesthesia from his surgery, and things were still foggy.

Roscoe was looking at Rogers but was talking to his partner, "You know Walsh, the party is over for this poor son of a bitch."

"How so?"

"Well, look at him. He only has two fingers on his right hand, he's going to have to wear that crap bag for the rest of his life and he has a divot on the side of his head the size of an avocado. Life in prison is bad enough when you're not a gimp, but this poor slob going to be in Hell for the rest of his life. Can you imagine every day of your life being bullied, beaten and abused?"

"Your right, Brown. I wouldn't wish that on a dog."

"Can you envision going to Attica looking like that? Craterhead, that's what they'll call him, craterhead. You just know some big greaser's going to make little Roger here his wife. Won't that be ironic, now he's going to be the wife who takes it from behind."

The fog was clearing out of Roger's brain; reality was starting to set in, what his future was going to be. He started to whimper and cry. "But King Solomon had 700 wives and 300 concubines"

Roscoe leaned close to Roger and whispered, "That's true, just remember what Solomon said Roger, happy wife, happy life."

"Really, I don't remember reading that in the Bible."

"It's in the small print."

Two years after Roger Rogers was out of the wheelchair and lost the colostomy bag. He pleaded not guilty to three counts of first-degree murder and two counts of kidnapping, plus some miscellaneous charges. After a six-week trial, he was found guilty of all charges and was sentenced to life without the possibility of parole and sent to Attica Prison.

Roger was taken to his cell where he was thrown in with a 280-pound gorilla, Sammy "the Butcher" White who was the leader of Attica's Aryan Brotherhood. The behemoth looked the new fish up and down; smiled and said, "Bend over, craterhead!"

The Case of the Dewy Decimal Demon

Captain O'Rourke called Detectives Brown and Walsh into his office.

"Sit down fellas. What's your caseload look like?"

Brown thought for a moment before answering. "Not too bad since we closed the case on Rogers. What's up Captain?"

"I got a letter from the family of Tommy Jackson, he was murdered back in '55. They're pleading for us to come up with something, anything. They're looking for some answers.

"Here's what I know in a nutshell, it looked like a home robbery gone bad. We think Jackson walked in on the robber, they fought, Jackson was tied up and then repeatedly stabbed, something like twenty-three times with a very unusual dagger or sword, something with a curved blade.

"Anyway, the original team worked on it for over four years and well, you know how things come up and it gets pushed further and further down the line until it's just another cold case."

"You want us to put a new set of eye's on it, Captain?" Walsh asked.

"I'd appreciate it, there's the case file, look it over and see what you can come up with."

Roscoe picked up the cardboard box full of notes, files, documents, reports, and photos.

"We'll look into it and let you know, Captain." Roscoe said as Walsh got the door.

"Hey Roscoe, you ever work on any cold case's before?"

"This is my first." Roscoe said as he started to organize the contents of Tommy Jackson's murder. "Let's try and see if we can systematize all this into some sort of coherent and intelligible mess."

It took the two of them three days to comb thru all the reports, files and evidence before they spoke a word to each other about the case.

"Where do you think we should start, Roscoe?"

"I'm thinking we should talk to the two detectives, Wilson and Foster, the coroner of record, then go back and re-interview all the friends, family and coworkers."

"Sounds good, I'll see where Wilson and Foster are these days and see when we can talk to them."

"Great, and I'll get hold of, let's see, Doctor Julius Wang. I think I heard he's over in the Bronx now. Hey, it's almost noon, I'll catch up with you an hour, I'm meeting Betty at Nathans for lunch."

"Roscoe, you eat there every day, they should make you a part owner."

"Hey, I'm a creature of habit, what can I tell you. You wanna come?"

"Naw, I'll grab something later, I'm going to try and get hold of Wilson and Foster. Give Betty a kiss for me."

Roscoe put on his fedora, trench coat and his picked up his umbrella and headed down to the boardwalk to meet Betty. He was old school, the hat and trench coat made him feel like a real New York City Detective, he could see a change in not only fashion in what the younger detectives were wearing but their hairstyles and even in their phraseology. Times were definitely changing and he knew that he'd have to change too or be left behind. But for him it would have to be gradual like he told Walsh, he was a creature of habit.

Betty was waiting outside of Nathans Famous Delicatessen talking to Vinnie the counterman when Roscoe arrived. He gave Betty a kiss and shook Vinnie's hand. Vinnie smiled and said, "We got worried that something happened to you, we were going to send out a search party. You're usually never late, everything okay?"

"Ha, Ha, very funny. Just for that I'm gonna have three chilidogs crinkle cut French fries, and soda pop, I'll show you, wise guy."

"Roscoe, you're such a rebel. Come on in you two, Betty what'll you have?"

"I'll have one hot dog mustard with relish and an orange soda."

Roscoe and Betty took their order over to the boardwalk and sat on a bench watching the people walking by, it was one of their favorite past times. They would try to deduce people's backgrounds and life stories by their appearance.

When he got back to the squad room Walsh was sitting at his desk eating a Nathans hotdog."

"What the? Why didn't you join Betty and me?"

"I would have felt like a third wheel, besides I was hunting down Wilson and Foster. I found them, they're at the one three, Manhattan South, we're scheduled to meet them tomorrow morning."

"You're a hell of a detective Jimmy Walsh. And I located our elusive Doctor Wang, he's living the good life over at the four two, Bronx."

"The Bronx?"

"Don't worry, he's agreed to come down here tomorrow afternoon. Any excuse to get out of the Bronx, I guess. The only good thing about the Bronx is the Yankees."

"I thought you were a Dodger fan."

"I was until them bums decided to move to LA. Can you imagine, of all places Los Angeles? They call Los Angeles the City of Angeles. I was there once; I didn't find it to be that exactly, although there are some nice people out there. I'm sorry, but both the Giants and Dodgers belong in Brooklyn. Used to be a game, now it's a business."

"Roscoe, let it go, they're gone and they're not coming back."

"Bums."

!! ⚫️🕯️☆🔥☠️⚡️ !!

Roscoe parked down the street from 230 East 21st Street, the thirteenth precinct station house. There was a parking spot in front of New York's Finest Police Gear and Equipment, purveyors of all things NYPD, holsters, official uniforms, saps, nightsticks, handcuffs, shoes, and caps. The only thing you can't buy is weapons or ammunition.

The store is owned and operated by Trevor Harrison, an ex-NYPD sergeant who was shot in the line of duty and became paralyzed from the waist down. Fellow officers come from all over the city to buy their gear and equipment from Trevor, even though there are places closer to many of the precincts. The place is always jumping from visiting New York's finest, some come to buy, some come to talk shop and some come just to kibitz.

Roscoe and Walsh ducked in to say hi before heading down to see Wilson and Foster.

"Trevor you old dog, how are you? Have you met my partner Jimmy Walsh, Jimmy this is Sergeant Harrison one of New York's finest."

"Pleasure to meet you Detective Walsh."

"The pleasure is mine, sir."

"What brings you down this why Roscoe?"

"Working a cold case, the murder of Tommy Jackson. It was Wilson and Fosters case originally now it's ours. Know anything about it?"

"Just that Wilson and Foster keep hitting brick walls, no evidence, no witnesses, no motive. Other than that, it was a slam dunk case."

"Great, now it's our turn. Well, we gotta run, it was great seeing you again. Hey, don't be such a lazy bum, wheel your ass over to Coney Island and I'll treat you to some dogs from Nathans."

"I just might do that. Good to meet you Walsh, you're welcome to stop by anytime, you don't need this bum to tag along."

"I will, I promise. Bye now."

Foster and Wilson's office was up on the fifth floor; they were prepared and waiting for the two Brooklyn Detectives. After the usual introductions and niceties, Wilson asked, "So, what's this all about?"

"Captain O'Rourke received a letter from the Jackson family inquiring about the case, so he asked us to put a fresh set of eyes on it." Roscoe told them.

"We collected our notes and provided a list of everyone we contacted." Foster said as he handed Walsh the paperwork.

Walsh asked, "Was there anyone suspect that you guys had a gut feeling was the killer?"

Both Wilson and Foster said that they thought Larry Sellers, Jackson's business partner was their lead suspect, but he had an alibi. His then-fiancée, Pamela Kurtz swore that they had spent the night together.

"Did they ever get married?" Roscoe asked.

"Married and recently divorced." Foster said.

"Well, I think we'll just have to have a little talk with the ex-Mrs. Sellers. Like they say, Hell hath no fury like a woman scorned. Right Walsh?"

"I wouldn't know, Roscoe."

Wilson stood as if to signal that the meeting was over, "If there's anything else we can help with. Just give us a shout."

On the ride back to the six O Walsh asked, "So what do think?"

"I think they are a little peeved that O'Rourke brought in two other detectives to work on their case. I know I would be cheesed off if it were my case."

"But, it doesn't mean that they're not good detectives, sometimes a case just needs a different perspective."

"I guess. So, let's see where we might find Larry's ex and see what she has to say."

On the drive back, Walsh reread Foster and Wilson's notes and reviewed the list of people that they talked to, there weren't that many, only six.

"There was Sellers, his fiancée, his three neighbors and Tommy's girlfriend, Janet Kenny."

"I personally think it had to be a man."

"Why a man?"

"Jackson was a big guy, I don't think a woman could have subdued him, tied those knots and then stabbed him twenty-three times. Although the multiple stabbings does have a ring of excess, that's a lot of times is a result of passion, hatred or both."

"Well, if you thinking a man did, there are only two men on the list, Sellers and a neighbor, Doug Williams, who lived next door to Jackson."

"What's his story?"

"Let's see, Doug Williams. At the time of Jackson's murder he was forty-four, he works in advertising as an account manager in Manhattan. An advertising agency called McCann-Erickson. He told police at the time of the murder he was alone in his apartment, said he heard some noise, but nothing that would have made him think that someone was being killed next door."

"What was it Jackson and Sellers did?"

"They had a public relations firm. Jackson was the business side and apparently, Sellers did the writing of press releases, crisis communications, mailers, news articles and promotional materials, junk like that."

"Did they find any clients that were pissed off?"

"Not according to this, most of their clients were non-profits like the Blood Bank and the Cancer Society, stuff like that, I don't really see those guys torturing and killing anyone."

"Let's start with Seller's ex, now that they're not married anymore she can testify against him.

The all brick apartment building at 2135 Homecrest Avenue was built before World War II, The rooms were much larger and with a ton more closet space than the cracker boxes that are built today, real wood floors, ten-foot ceilings, crown-molding, solidly built and made to last.

They found number 616, Roscoe rang the doorbell.

"Pamela Sellers?"

"I was, I'm actually going by my maiden name Kurtz."

"Ms. Kurtz, I'm Detective Brown and this is my partner, Detective Walsh. We were hoping you might have a few minutes to talk to us."

"Of course, please come in."

Pamela Kurtz was an attractive woman in her middle fifties, dark auburn hair worn that she wore in a Bouffant that gave her a Jackie Kennedy look, and she was dressed to the nines wearing designer clothes of Paco Rabanne.

The apartment was nicely furnished with expensive antiques, the furniture felt a little too heavy for Roscoe's taste. Most of the wood was made of dark mahogany, the sofa and chairs overstuffed, the windows were surrounded on either side with Italian drapes made from wool, Persian and oriental rugs, and dozens of early French landscape paintings hanging on the walls. The environment was that of a museum rather than a home, he was expecting to see signs telling you not to sit on or touch anything.

"May I get you gentlemen anything to drink?"

"No thank you, we won't take too much of your time, we just have a few questions."

"Please do sit down. Now, what can I do for you?"

"We've been asked to go back and look into the death of Tommy Jackson."

"Like I told the original officers, my husband and I were here at the time of Tommy's death."

"Yes ma'am, and you're certain your husband never left the apartment?"

"Well, Detective Brown, it was a long time ago, nine years I believe. I suppose when we went to bed after I fell asleep he could have slipped out of the apartment. I am a very heavy sleeper, you see. But to my knowledge, he was here with me."

"So, he could leave the apartment and you not know it."

"It's possible."

"Had he ever gotten out of bed and left the apartment while you were asleep before?"

"A couple times."

"And what did he say he went when this occurred?"

"He said that he sometimes had to go to the office because he had to finish some copy or a finalize a press release up. And a couple of times he went down to see Tommy about a client."

"What time would you and Mr. Sellers usually go to sleep?"

"We were usually in bed by eleven, we use to watch the news and then Johnny Carson."

"I see, and Mr. Jackson's apartment was just down the hall is that correct?"

"Yes, he was in 635, down the hall and on the other side of the building."

"Ms. Kurtz, when you were interviewed by the police before, you were pretty emphatic that your husband didn't leave the apartment that night and now you're saying that it was a possibility, why the change?"

"Well, Detective Brown divorce has a way of sharpening one's memory."

"Ms. Kurtz, I have to ask you, were you telling the truth then or are you telling the truth now?"

"If I were to swear on a Bible, I'd say now."

"Thank you, Ms. Kurtz, we appreciate your time. Can you tell us where we might find your ex-husband?"

She stood up, walked over to a French writing desk, picked up an envelope and handed it to Roscoe, "The return address is Larry's, you can keep the envelope, I already took the alimony check out of it."

Roscoe folded the envelope and placed it into his inside coat jacket, "Would you mind telling me why you got divorced?"

"I caught him in our bed with another woman. So, I took him for every penny he had."

"How long have you been divorced?"

"Ten glorious months."

Walsh said, "Well, he's number one on my top ten list, how about you?"

"Yeah, he's heading the charts at number one. He has the means, possibly the opportunity, but we need the motive. And, we still have to check out the others just to be sure. Who's next?"

Doug Williams had been Jackson's next-door neighbor for the six years that Tommy had lived in the building. He had an airtight alibi; he was in Los Angeles shooting a television commercial for Philco Televisions.

He stated that there were a few times that he heard yelling and doors slamming at Tommy's apartment and they all involved his partner, Larry Sellers. He admitted that the walls are thick and he couldn't make out what the arguments were about, but there was definitely shouting coming from Tommy's apartment.

The other two neighbors had both passed away, they were an elderly couple in their eighties nine years ago, even if they were alive there was no way they could have committed the murder.

The last person to interview aside from Sellers was Tommy's girlfriend at the time, Janet Kenny, currently Janet Singer. Walsh and Roscoe found her living in Manhattan Beach at 145 Mackenzie, a small brick single dwelling. From the outside it was kept very tidy, in the driveway was a Ford station wagon and out front of the house was a tricycle and miscellaneous, she was married with a little boy.

"Excuse me ma'am, I'm Detective Brown and this is my partner Detective Walsh, would you be Janet Singer?"

"Yes, has something happened to Charles?"

"No. We didn't mean to alarm you, we're looking into the death of Tommy Jackson and we understand that you were seeing him at the time. May we come in?"

"Yes, but please be quiet, I just got my son to sleep for his nap. Let's go into the kitchen."

They walked thru the house to the back where the kitchen was located. She invited them to sit at the kitchen table and offered them some coffee, they declined.

The inside of the house had the telltale signs of a young child, toys strewn around, messed up tabletops and of course tiny handprints on the furniture and walls.

Roscoe decided to let Walsh take the lead on the questioning of Janet Singer. He was closer to her age and had a way with the ladies.

"Mrs. Singer, you were Mr. Jackson's girlfriend at the time of his death, is that correct?"

"Yes, we had been dating for a little over a year, when he was killed."

"Was it serious?"

"Well like I said, we had only been seeing each other for about a year, for me, it was still too early to tell where the relationship was going. But, I can honestly say I cared for Tommy very much. I was crushed when I was told of his death."

"Can you think of anyone who might have wanted to do Tommy any harm?"

"I believe that I told the police who interviewed me all those years ago that I couldn't think of anyone who might have wanted to hurt Tommy. There should be a record of what I said back then."

"Oh there is, my partner and I are putting a fresh set of eyes on the case, plus you know sometimes people remember things years later that they may have forgotten or repressed at the time of the tragedy."

She sat across from them staring outside into the tiny backyard thinking for several minutes.

Walsh asked, "Were there any times that he ever had arguments or disagreements with anyone, clients, neighbors, his partner?"

"Towards the end, he did complain about Larry, his partner. I had met Larry only a couple of times, but I didn't care for him, he seemed to me to always try to skim and scam the clients. To me he was like a snake oil salesman, know what I mean. There's nothing specific it was just a feeling.

There were times Tommy would tell me that they occasionally really got into to shouting matches, but overall Tommy tried to keep his business life out of our relationship. I don't know if that helps."

"It does, well we won't take up any more of your time, here is my card, if you happen to remember anything, no matter how trivial you think it is, please contact me."

"Nice work, Jimmy. Now, all we have to do is find, Mr. Sellers."

"Let's head back to the precinct and see if there's any news."

!! 💣🕆🔆🍃🐢🎋🗲!!

"Mr. Sellers? Mr. Larry Sellers?"

"Yes, I'm Larry Sellers, can I help you?"

"This is Detective Brown, I'm calling you in regard to the death of your business partner Mr. Thomas Jackson. I was wondering if you might have a few moments to speak with me?"

"Over the phone?"

"Actually I was hoping that you could come down to the 60th precinct or if that's inconvenient I could come and speak with you at your home. What would be most convenient for you, sir?"

"Could you tell why you want to speak to me, Tommy's death was almost ten years ago."

"Well sir, it's just that we're trying to put this case to rest and we just need to tie up a couple loose ends and could really appreciate your help. What do you say?"

"Alright, where are you located?"

"We're at 2951 West 8th Street, Brooklyn."

"Geez, that's all the way down in Coney Island."

"Well, if it would be more convenient for you like I said we could come to you."

"You know maybe that would be better. 138 East 38th Street, Murray Hill, it's the Catham House. I'm in 8B, B as in boy."

"Very good, and would this evening be good for you sir?"

"Yeah, I'll be home at six, so any time after six-thirty. It's not a doorman building, so just buzz me and I'll let you in."

"Excellent, I look forward to meeting with you. Goodbye."

Roscoe hung up the phone and gave a big thumbs up to Walsh sitting on the office couch, reading the New York Post. Roscoe smiled, rubbed his hands together and said, "Six-thirty, 38th, and Lex."

Walsh parked the police car in a tow-away zone in front of Seller's building; he folded down the driver's side sun visor that had a handwritten sign, "POLICE ON DUTY" attached with two rubber bands. They walked into the glass-enclosed foyer and rang the buzzer for 8B.

"Who is it?" squawked the intercom speaker.

"Detective Brown."

A loud buzzing sound seemed to be coming from the glass door and with one tug of the handle they were in the lobby, the elevator was awaiting them with doors open, they took the short ride to the 8th floor. The doors slowly opened and staring them in the face was a plastic sign alerting them that apartments A, B, C, and D were to their left.

The door to apartment 8B was slightly opened, Roscoe gave a quick knock and the two detectives entered the apartment, Larry Sellers was sitting in an overstuffed armchair with a book in his hand.

The apartment was sparsely decorated, minimal furniture and a few posters on the walls, Roscoe had seen the fallout from the property battles of divorces, usually the woman ends up with the apartment or home with the majority of the furnishings while the man has to start from scratch, unless there's another woman that he moves in with.

"Do come in and make your self's comfortable."

They sat on the couch opposite Sellers, Roscoe took off his hat and placed it on the coffee table, "Do you mind?"

"Not at all Detective."

"Mr. Sellers, I'm Detective Brown I spoke with you earlier, and this is my partner Detective Walsh, first I want to thank you for taking the time to meet with us."

"Well, I just hope I can be of some help."

"As I mentioned, we're trying to finally close the case and we just need a couple questions answered."

"Of course."

"You were Mr. Jackson's business partner."

"That's right, Tommy and I had a public relations firm, he ran the administrative and client side of the business and I was basically the creative department, writing press releases, speeches and things of that nature."

"How long were you partners?"

"About five years, before he was killed."

"What happened to the business when Mr. Jackson was killed?"

"The company closed, I didn't have the head for the business side, and so I just closed up shop."

"Did you go work for another PR firm?"

"Actually no. I took what equality that was in the business and tried my hand at writing novels."

"Novels, what kind of novels?"

"Oh, murder mysteries."

"Really, I read a ton of murder mystery's and don't think I've seen any books by Larry Sellers."

"Well, actually I write under the name of Arcy Koala."

"Arcy Koala yeah, you wrote "The Girl In Red", I read that, that was pretty good. Parts were a little unreal, but overall pretty good."

"Well, thank you Detective, that means a lot coming from someone like you."

"What else have you written?"

"I have two new ones, "The Devil Wears Black" and "Death Of A Stranger.""

"I'll have to read them. Now, on the night of his death, I understand you had an argument."

"Detective Brown, Tommy and my relationship was complicated, our business relationship was a rocky, lots of ups and downs. That was business, but our friendship was even. We would argue over the business, but it never crept into our personal friendship."

"Did you have anything to do with the death of Mr. Jackson?"

"No."

"Your ex-wife now says that she can't swear that you two spend the entire evening together."

"I'm not surprised, we had a contentious divorce Detective and we're still fighting over a couple of things."

"So, did Mr. Jackson have any enemy's that you know of? Clients, friends, or neighbors?"

"None that I knew of."

"Okay, Mr. Sellers we'll be in touch if there's anything else we need. Here's my card, call me if you think of anything."

"I will."

On the way back to the precinct Roscoe and Walsh stopped off at 828 Broadway, downtown Manhattan. The Strand Book store to pick up copies of The Devil Wears Black and Death Of A Stranger. Roscoe thought he died and went to heaven every time he went to the Strand, the bookstore has been around since 1927 and proclaims it has over eighteen miles of books, a readers paradise.

"Jimmy, why don't you read The Devil Wears Black and I'll read Death Of A Stranger."

"And we're reading them because?"

"What, you got something better to do?"

"Maybe."

"Like what?"

"There's a new "Bonanza" on tonight, and it's in color."

"Well, I wouldn't want you to miss such a cultured event."

"But, it's in color."

Roscoe got home around seven that evening; Betty was waiting dinner for him. She had made his favorite, meatloaf, mashed potatoes and peas with mushrooms, he called it comfort food. After dinner they settled in for the evening, listening to WQXR, classical radio and reading. Betty agreed to read one of Sellers books, although she wasn't a big fan of murder mysteries. She chose The Devil Wears Black, so Roscoe took Death Of A Stranger.

Both Roscoe and Betty were voracious readers, reading two to three books a week on average. Sellers murder novels would be fast reads, each book was only two hundred and fifty pages.

After finishing The Devil Wears Black Betty said, "Hmm, the story was simplistic, the dialogue cheesy and the plot had holes the size of a truck you could drive thru, but overall it was a fun read. And how was yours?"

Roscoe peered over the book, "Excellent."

"Larry Sellers you're under arrest for the murder of Tommy Jackson." Roscoe said as Detective Walsh put the handcuffs on him.

"You're making a big mistake, Detectives." Sellers protested as the two detectives escorted him out of the 5th Avenue Barnes & Noble during a book signing of Death Of A Stranger.

"You know Mr. Sellers, you've only yourself and Arcy Koala to blame."

"What are you talking about?"

"Death Of A Stranger, the murder of Harold Jenkins describes the murder details of Tommy Jackson to a tee. Even down to the exact details of the type of knots, you used to tie Jackson up with, and even the kris dagger that was used to stab him with. We have search warrants for your car, your apartment, and your prior residence, in your book you tell where you hid the murder weapon. You wouldn't be that stupid to actually hide it there, would you Larry?"

"I don't know what you're talking about, Death Of A Stranger is fiction, I made it all up."

"We'll see."

Back at the police station they placed Mr. Sellers in interview room 3 and started the interrogation.

Walsh brought in the Jackson file and sat down across from Sellers, Roscoe followed him in carrying three cups of coffee. He placed a cup in front of each of them and sat down.

"Detective, this is ridiculous. Death Of A Stranger is pure fiction."

Roscoe held the copy of Death Of A Stranger and opened it to page 188 and started to read, "Roger then took a four-foot length of rope that he had brought to Jenkins's apartment and proceeded to tie him up, using a Tom fool's knot, which is considered a handcuff knot. Detective Walsh, what kind of knot was used to tie Tommy Jackson up with?"

"Tom fools knot."

Roscoe then turned to page 192, "Roger reached behind his back and pulled out the ceremonial dagger that he purchased while on vacation in Bali, a jewel-encrusted handled ten-inch blade kris, distinctive for its wavy blade. Detective Walsh, what kind of knife was used to stab Tommy Jackson?"

"Ten-inch blade kris."

There was a knock on the interview room door, Officer Beech entered the room and handed a note to Roscoe, who read it and turned to page 210, "Once the deed was done Roger went back to his apartment and silently opened the front door so as not disturb his sleeping wife. Needing to hide the murder weapon he slid the dagger into the large pot that held the grandiose Ficus plant in the apartments entranceway. Detective Walsh, would you please the note that was just brought in please?"

"A knife was found hidden inside of a large plant pot in the entranceway of Mrs. Sellers apartment."

"Think we'll find Tommy Jackson's blood on that knife, Mr. Sellers?"

"Just my luck, a literate cop."

"Sorry to disappoint you Mr. Sellers, but we're not all Neanderthals. Book 'em, Walsh."

"Very funny, copper."

M. Ward Leon

The Case of Never Odd Or Even

Hauptmann Level Reittier rose quickly thru the ranks of Hitler's Wehrmacht, in 1939 he was asked if he wanted to transfer over into the prestigious Waffen-SS and of course, he did. Lehel was a good little Nazi, as was his blond wife Elle and his blue-eyed, pure Aryan son Otto, who at the tender age of fourteen joined the Hitlerjugend, the Hitler Youth and soon became a shining star. He was one of only sixteen boys who rose to the rank of Reichsjugendfüher, a National Youth Leader out of eight million.

Otto was totally committed to the Party, people who knew him said that he was even more Hitler than Hitler with his hate for any other races other than the Aryan Race, especially the Jews. One of his favorite pass times was he would walk the streets of Berlin with a group of fellow Hitlerjugends with an American baseball bat resting on his shoulder and whenever he saw a person wearing a yellow star of David sewn on their clothes, be it man, woman or child bash their brains in with his Louisville Slugger as his troops would cheer him on, he then would carve a notch in the handle. It was rumored that he had over thirty notches on his bat when the war started.

By the time the Germans stormed into Poland twenty-year-old Otto Reittier had earned the rank of Oberleutnant and like his father, joined the Waffen-SS. Like most members of the Waffen-SS, Otto was involved in numerous atrocities thru out Europe. His brutality didn't go unnoticed by none other than Gruppenfüher Richard Glücks, the Concentration Camps Inspectorate. Glücks oversaw all the concentration camps in Europe and handpicked Otto Reittier to supervise the highly profitable theft of cash and assets from the Holocaust victims as they entered the death camps. It was Otto's bright idea to sell slave labor to private companies, which got him promoted to the rank of Hauptmann, the same rank as his father.

As they say, with great power comes great responsibility, Otto loved his work and looked forward every day in the killing of the enemies of the Reich.

Hauptmann Lehel Reittier never knew of his son's rapid rise thru the ranks, he was killed by a group of French resistance fighters while strolling the streets of Paris. His mother was killed when the Allies bombed Dresden. Otto had little time for sympathy; he had too many Jews to kill and so little time.

But he did plenty of enough time to become a wealthy man by the use of judicial and creative bookkeeping. He opened several Swiss bank accounts and had several major works of art smuggled out of Germany for safekeeping.

When the writing was on the wall that the allies were going to be victorious, Otto deserted and silently made his way to Switzerland. From there he worked his way thru the Odessa underground to Buenos Aires, Argentina under the name Robert Trebor.

Robert Trebor was offered a job as a plant manager for IG Farben, the company that manufactured Zyklon B, the poison gas used in the Nazi gas chambers. He worked in Buenos Aires until his request for immigration to the United States was approved in 1957.

Trevor had a Vice President position in New York City with the Bayer Corporation waiting for him, which was a division of IG Farben during the war. He was to be in charge of the Bayer Aspirin account, it is rumored that Arthur Eichengrun, a German Jew, founded aspirin, however, the Nazis couldn't give credit to a Jew, so they gave the credit to a nice Aryan fellow, Felix Hoffman.

By the time Otto Reittier aka Robert Trebor stepped off Pan Am flight 1331 he had changed his appearance by growing a full bread, dying his blond hair brown, wearing nonprescription horned rim glasses and toned down his German accent. He was now ready to become an American, a racist, bigoted, and anti-Semitic American, but an American, nonetheless.

Anna Eseese had finally gotten her wish, after training to become an OP-Schwester, an operating theatre nurse she was being assigned to a quaint little hospital just 56 miles from Berlin in Ravensbrück concentration camp.

Ravensbrück was a concentration camp exclusively for women. The women prisoners were Jews, gypsies, women involved in the resistance, and asocials, women who didn't measure up to the norms of the National Socialist vision of Volksgemeinschaft or community standards.

The hospital, which was known, as the Revier was ill-equipped with proper medical supplies as the troops on the front were given top priority. Soon, like all the other nurse and doctors Anna looked upon the misery and anguish of the sick and dying with indifference and at times sarcasm. Of the 130,000 prisoners that were imprisoned only 15,000 survived by the end of the war.

Anna had administered lethal injections to prisoners who she deemed unfit for work, she also willingly participated in experiments that entailed creating an artificial wound and then infecting the women with foreign materials to see the efficacy of sulfonamide drugs, which they knew in advance would have no effect.

In 1945 when the Russians were advancing from the East and were poised to capture Ravensbrück, Anna decided it was time to leave and she did. She made her way to where the Americans lines were and blended in as a refugee, she changed her last name to Lagerregal, Anna Lagerregal. Her identification she stole from a prisoner from the camp who she personally had given a lethal injection for no other reason than the woman resembled her, which meant her identity papers weren't forged like so many other war criminals that got caught with phony papers.

Anna Lagerregal followed the same route to America, as did Robert Trebor, Germany, Switzerland, and Argentina to America. But unlike Otto Reittier, Anna did nothing to change her identity; she wore her long blond hair as she did in the camp. She did, however, use makeup to cover the Blutgruppentätowierung, blood type tattoo under her left arm that all Waffen-SS soldiers were required to have. When she went through the screening of the Allies of all German citizens, she was amazed how easy it was to fool them, the Americans were so overwhelmed by the sheer number of people and the chaos that she just skated thru the process and was on her way.

When Anna Lagerregal arrived in New York she was greeted by an Odessa member who got her set up in an apartment in lower Manhattan and a job as a nurse at Bellevue Hospital in Orthopedics.

!! 👊✝☆🔱💀❋⚡ !!

1965, Lyndon Johnson was sworn in for a full term as President, Bloody Sunday in Selma, Alabama, the Vietnam War was starting to heat up and Roscoe Brown and Betty Armstrong tied the knot in June, love, and hate was in the air.

Later that year another marriage took place, a much grander wedding than that of Roscoe and Betty, it was the wedding of Anna Lagerregal and Robert Trebor, a more beautiful couple couldn't be found in all of Manhattan. They looked like two Aryans from Darien, by this time Otto decided it was safe to save off his beard, but he did keep dying his hair, after all, it would be hard to explain at the office. The marriage made all the society columns, the NY Times, the Daily News and even Page 6 in the Post.

Unlike Roscoe and Betty, who honeymooned a long weekend in lovely Atlantic City, the Trebors spent two glorious weeks on the sandy beaches of Tahiti. Yes, the Trebors were a match made in heaven, Nazi heaven.

Although Otto and Anna were poster children for European immigration, they gave the outward appearance of the All-American couple unlike all the vile refugee riffraff coming in from third world countries that would be polluting our pure gene pool something had to be done, so they joined the National States' Rights Party and were anonymous donors to the American Nazi Party.

To show his appreciation, George Lincoln Rockwell, the founder of the American Nazi Party hosted a dinner in their honor held at the Plaza Hotel. It was that dinner party that would prove to be their undoing, for not only was the FBI and the NYPD surveilling the event, but there were also several members from the group known as Nakam, a group of fifty odd Holocaust survivors who sought to reap revenge upon Germans and Nazis.

They went beyond an eye for an eye; they wanted to kill six million Germans, a nation for a nation. One of their plans was to plant large quantities of poison to the water system in the city of Nuremburg, but their plans were foiled. The majority of the members were in Europe, only a handful members were in the United States whose goal was to assassinate known Nazis, particularly members of the Waffen-SS. Particularly the Ken and Barbie of the Nazi Party.

!! 💀✝☆🌿🕸️⚡!!

Arbeit Macht Frei, Work Sets You Free was the sign that prisoners saw as they entered the Auschwitz death camp. Emme Nenonen was 18 in 1943 when she and her family were brought to the camp. Of the twelve members of her family who entered the camp, only she was able to survive.

They arrived in the middle of the night after spending eight days traveling in a cattle car with no food or water, they couldn't lie down, there wasn't room. The cars were so tightly packed that they had to sleep standing up. Once they got to Auschwitz and were unloaded, dozens of people were discovered to have died standing upright.

Guards yelling, snarling dogs barking, the whole scene seemed to be total chaos, but for the Nazis, it was well planned and organized chaos designed to keep people dazed and confused. Emme witnessed her older sister's six-month-old baby being torn from her arms by an SS guard because it was crying, he grabbed the baby by the feet and swung it around so its head was smashed against a corner of a brick building three times, then just dropped it on the ground and walked away.

Once Emme made it passed the Angel of Death, Doctor Josef Mengele who had the power of life and death by selecting those who would work and those who would be sent to the gas chambers, she was made to strip naked, have her head shaven, relieved herself of any jewelry or valuables, and then issued the paper thin stripped prison uniform that countless others had worn before her.

Her mornings would start at 4:30 a.m. with roll call that would last until 7:00, standing outside rain or shine while the guards would force them to squat with their hands above their heads for an hour, or while guards would dole out beatings for minor infractions.

After roll call, they were marched out of camp to work nonstop for 12 hours at construction sites, gravel pits and lumber yards, six days a week. That was her life for two years; Emme weighed 125 pounds when she arrived at Auschwitz, she weighed 60 pounds when the Allies rescued her.

Emme spent the next three years in and out of internment camps looking for any members of her family that survived, none did. She finally received sponsorship from an uncle living in New York City, having escaped Germany in 1938 before the doors were permanently shut for Jews.

!!☀︎†☼⚐☠︎❁⚡︎!!

On October 5th, 1955 Emme arrived in New York where she was welcomed by her Uncle Levi and her Aunt Ester who had a small apartment in Manhattan's lower East side. Levi Nenonen had a small tailor shop where he would do alterations, repairs, and piecework for people in the garment district. Emme worked in her uncle's tailor shop running errands, delivering finished pieces and doing minor alterations.

One Saturday while returning home from synagogue she met a young man, Navan Renner a New York City cab driver and a fellow survivor of Auschwitz who was a member of Nakam. Over the next couple months they became lovers, but since their past experiences during the war, they felt no compulsion for any long term plans like marriage, they lived each day as if it were to be their last. They did move in together into his house on Mermaid Avenue in Coney Island.

One day in 1965 Navan saw the wedding announcement of Anna Lagerregal and Robert Trebor, both who were on the kill list of Nakam for crimes against humanity. He showed Emme the announcement from the New York Times and of his plan to kidnap and kill the two ex-Waffen SS officers, he told her so she could walk away and not get caught up in what he was going to do, but to his surprise she wanted to participate, hoping that this would bring her some form of closure.

Nava drove his cab exclusively in and around their neighborhood on the upper West side in hopes of picking them up as a fare. For eight months, nothing, until one September weekend they were standing on the corner of West 102nd Street and West End Avenue trying to hail a cab.

"Would you be able to take us to the New York Aquarium in Coney Island, there's a fundraising event we have to attend. I'll make it worth your while." Otto pleaded.

"You bet, hop in."

Navan had a special switch to lock the back cab doors so his prey couldn't escape, he had the back windows tinted so people couldn't see in and installed a heavy-duty wire mesh screen so no one could violate his space.

The blond smiled and said, "You're a life saver, our usual car service is having personal problems. I think it has something to do with their union, it's very inconvenient for sure."

Otto looked at Navan's hack license and asked, "Renner, is that Jewish?"

"Jewish? No, it's French, pronounced René. My parents immigrated to America in the twenties."

"Were you in the war?"

"Yeah, I caught the tail end of it, I was in the Navy, stationed in Guam. You?"

"Army, I was mostly in Germany."

"Wow, that must have been rough duty. I hear those fucking Nazis put up a really good fight." Navan said peering into the rearview mirror looking for a reaction but got none.

"Yeah, it was rough, they were really tough and dedicated to that Führer."

"I hear old Schicklgruber weened out and wacked himself rather than going out like a real man. You were there whatda think?" Navan saw that this got a bit of a rise out of the bastard.

Otto and Anna were so engrossed in the conversation and Nazi bashing that they didn't realize until it was too late that they were pulling inside a small house's garage.

"Where the hell are we?" Otto shouted as they tried to open the cab doors, to no avail.

"Let us out of here at once!" Anna ordered.

The Trebor's weren't use to not having their orders obeyed; after all, they were part of the master race.

Emme walked into the garage from the house carrying a gun that she handed to Navan The gun was a tranquilizer gun, he fired two darts, one into each of his fares. It took less than a minute for the drug to take effect. Soon the Trebors found themselves lying naked on the cold garage floor with the hands and feet bound tight and a rope around each of their necks.

!! 🖤✝☆🔨💀✖⚡!!

"What the Hell is going on here?" Otto shouted.

"I'll tell you Herr Reittier, it's called revenge." Navan replied as he helped Reittier and Anna to their knees.

"You must have me mistaken for someone else, my name is Robert Trebor, not Reittier."

"And you were never in the Waffen-SS?"

"No never."

"Then can you explain the Blutgruppentätowierung on your arm, Herr Reittier? And yours Fräulein Eseese?"

"My name is Anna Lagerregal, and that isn't a blood type tattoo it's a birthmark."

"How did you know that Blutgruppentätowierung is a blood type tattoo, Fräulein Eseese?" Navan asked.

Anna quickly answered, "My parents are German, but we lived in Milwaukee on a small dairy farm.

"Really, I have an Aunt and Uncle from Milwaukee. How long did you live there?" Navan inquired.

"I grew up there."

"Okay then, what is the name of the famous statue of an American revolutionary hero, mounted on his horse in Lincoln Village?"

"Abraham Lincoln."

"I'm afraid not Fräulein Eseese, the answer is actually kind of ironic, because of all the atrocities you Nazis heaped upon the Polish people, the one answer that could have saved your life was Tedeusz Kosciuszko, a Polish military leader."

"Scheisse! Verdammte Juden!"

Navan pulled on the ropes around the captive's neck forcing them to stand up. Anna showed anger and contempt, Otto was more stoic.

Emme walked up to Otto and slapped him hard across the face and said in a cold and detached voice, "1943, Auschwitz death camp, my family arrived late in the evening, my older sister was holding her 6-month-old baby girl, Hannah who was crying. You walked up to my sister and snatched the infant out of her arms and coldly walked over and smashed her head against a brick wall several times. You then dropped its lifeless body on the ground and just walked away."

Emme spits in his face and nodded to Navan, who slowly pulled the rope around Otto's neck until his toes were just an inch off the ground. Emme stood in front of him passionless and watched him slowly die.

Anna tried to resist, begging for mercy, but there was none to be had. After they were both dead, Navan took a tattoo gun and tattooed their German names, their ranks and their crimes on their stomachs. Navan also tattooed a Star of David on their upper left chest where Jews were forced to wear the yellow star on their clothes.

Late that night around 3 a.m. Navan and Emme took the bodies to Asser Levy Park in Coney Island and hung their bodies next to each other from a lone Maple tree at the east end of the park. Navan thought it only fitting that these two Nazi war criminals should be hung in a park named after a Jew.

Once they were safely away, they drove up to Crown Heights and anonymously called all the local television stations, the New York Times, the Daily News and the Post, then they phoned the police department telling everyone that it was the work of the group called Nakam, which means "Revenge" in Hebrew.

At 4:00 a.m. Detective Sergeant Roscoe Brown got a call that there are two dead naked Nazis hanging from a tree in Asser Levy Park. As he gets out of bed, Betty asks, "What's going on?"

"Just a couple of naked dead hanging around Asser Levy Park, now go back to sleep."

When Roscoe met his partner Detective Jimmy Walsh at Levy Park at 4:45 a.m. the place was a media madhouse, the uniform officers were in a battle scrum with newspaper photographers, local TV camera crews and reporters of every size, shape, and nationality all jockeying for position. The place was lit up like Yankee Stadium, The CSI boys had to literally fight their way through the throngs of onlookers, freaks and both pro and anti-Nazi groups, it was really a three ring circus. Barnum and Bailey had nothing on this freak show.

Roscoe and Walsh approached Officer Travis Weir, who was the first to respond to the call.

"Hey T, what do we have?" Roscoe asked.

"Well me and my partner Harris were getting ready to go off duty when we got a call that there were these two dead Nazis hanging from a tree in Levy Park. When we got here we found a bunch of these news guys all over the place taking pictures, and stepping all over the crime scene, so me and Harris started some knocking heads trying to maintain as much evidence as we could."

"Anybody hurt?"

"Naw, maybe a few of these bums got a bit of a headache, but we didn't draw blood or nothing like that."

"Okay, good job, anybody gives you any grief, you have them come see me, now go sign out."

"Thanks, Roscoe."

"Okay, Jimmy let's take a look at what we got."

It was obvious to the two detectives that the killing took place somewhere else and then the bodies moved here. The tattooing was crude and looked like it had been done after the victims were dead. There wasn't any evidence anywhere in the surrounding area, and if there had been with all the unauthorized traffic roaming around it was either contaminated or gone.

Roscoe had Walsh copy the verbiage of the tattoos so they could go back to the station and do a background check on these two supposed Nazis.

!! 🎅†☼🌿☠✳⚡!!

"Naked Nazis Swaying in the Park" was the headline for the morning edition of the Daily News. It was the lead story in every paper, every TV station, and every call-in radio program, it even led off all the major networks newscasts. So, it was no surprise that Captain O'Rourke was waiting for Roscoe and Walsh when they returned to the precinct, "What do ya have?" O'Rourke asked Roscoe.

"Not much, I would say the chances of us finding any usable physical evidence would be slim to none. The crime scene looked like the Macy's Christmas parade marched thru the park.

"It will be a couple hours before the ME sends down his report. Jim and I are going to get in touch with the Simon Wiesenthal Center when they open to see if in fact, these two were Nazis, after all, meanwhile were checking out this group Nakam, who is claiming responsibility for the hanging.

"So, basically we're just getting started, Captain."

"Okay, thanks, Roscoe. This has become a real hot potato, everybody from the police commissioner on up are wanting results, the news outlets are relentless."

"We understand, but it has to be done right."

"Right, keep me posted. Oh, and if there's anything you need just shout."

"Thanks, Captain."

They two detectives went back into Roscoe's office to try and start to piece this case together.

Roscoe plopped down in his chair and rubbed his eyes, it was going to be a long day and not an easy one.

"So Jimmy, how's about you go and check out the what you can find out about our victims, you know friends, neighbors, coworkers and I'll see what I can find out about this Nakam outfit?" Roscoe looked at his watch and said, "And we'll meet at their apartment tonight at six. Whatta say?"

"Sounds like a plan."

Walsh went back to his desk and started making phone calls, first to Robert Trebor's place of employment, the Bayer Corporation to set up an appointment to come and talk to Trebor's boss and coworkers and then take a look around in his office. Next, he contacted Bellevue Hospital to arrange for an appointment to speak to Anna Lagerregal's coworkers and supervisors.

Roscoe decided just to go over to the Wiesenthal Center in Manhattan and not call, he was never comfortable on the phone, he was an 'in the moment' kinda guy.

Since Walsh had to go into Manhattan too, they decided that Walsh should drive and drop Roscoe off at the Wiesenthal Center downtown near Battery Park, then take the car over to Kips Bay to Bellevue Hospital, then to the West side near Columbus Circle to Bayer headquarters and finally to the Trebor's apartment, 299 W. 102nd Street where he would meet up with Roscoe at six.

!!�☆⚓☠✵⚡!!

Roscoe walked into the lobby of 11 Broadway, went straight to the elevator bank and rode to the seventh floor to Suite 766. The office wasn't what he had expected, it was one small room with six people working in cramped conditions, every desk had stacks and stacks of papers and folders piled on top, some of the people were talking on the phone while others were busy clacking away on typewriters which made for a very chaotic environment. A man from the back of the office shouted out, "Can we help you?"

Roscoe held up his badge and said, "I'm Detective Brown, is there someone I could talk to, it's about the murder of two suspected Nazis in Levy Park."

The room went very quiet, the kind of you could hear yourself breath quiet. The man walked up to where Roscoe was and held out his hand, "Detective, I am David Adleman, "How may I help you?"

"Mr. Adleman, we have two murder victims that we suspect might have been members of the SS, and I was hoping that you might be able to confirm if they actually were."

"We would be glad to help you in any way we can. What are their names?"

"Otto Reittier and Anna Eseese."

"Why don't you have a seat Detective on the sofa here and I'll be right back." Adleman said as he walked back to his desk, opened a large black book and started to thumb thru it.

The office slowly began to come back to life, papers began shuffling, typewriters began clacking and phones started ringing, chaos was up and running once again.

Roscoe sat patiently watching the office ballet being performed in front of him, for such a small office he could tell that they must have worked together many years to operate so seamlessly.

David Adleman returned with a couple Xerox pages and handed them to Roscoe.

"Otto Reittier and Anna Eseese were both officers in the Waffen-SS. Otto Reittier was a Hauptmann or Captain assigned to the Concentration Camps Inspectorate, he was handpicked to supervise the theft of cash and assets from the Holocaust victims as they entered the death camps. Otto Reittier arranged to sell slave labor to private companies. He was considered to be the golden boy, a shining star destined to rise to the top. Himmler was actually grooming him to be his number two and possible successor."

"Sounds like a real sweetheart of a guy."

"Anna Eseese worked as a nurse, and I use the term lightly at Ravensbrück Concentration Camp for women. As a nurse, she administered lethal injections to prisoners who she deemed unfit for work. Anna Eseese also was a willing participant in experiments that created artificial wounds in women and then infecting them with foreign materials to see the effect of how long before the infections would kill them."

"Nice. Just the kind of girl you want to bring home to meet mother."

Adleman asked, "How did they die if you don't mind my asking?"

"Don't mind at all, they were hung, and left hanging in Levy Park in Coney Island naked from a Maple tree. Someone had tattooed their names and pseudo names on their stomachs along with some other information."

"That's terrible."

"Why terrible? They were the scum of the earth."

"It's terrible because they should have stood trial so the world could see what evil people they were and expose all the evil that they did."

"There is a group claiming responsibility, Nakam. Ever heard of them."

"Ah Nakam, was a group of about fifty Holocaust survivors that tried to exact revenge against the German people by poisoning the water supplies of Nuremberg. They were wanting to kill six million Germans as revenge for the six million Jews that were killed in the camps. Their plan was foiled and they were all captured. That was right after the war, so whoever did this was probably someone or a group of people just using the name Nakam. I doubt if any of the original members were involved, most of the surviving members eventually went to Israel."

"Is it possible to get the names of the original members, if it's not then maybe it could be a relative here in New York."

"That will take some time to get."

"Here is my card, give me a call if you have anything and I'll come by and get it."

"I might have something for by tomorrow if that's okay."

"That's fine Mr. Adleman, by the way, what does Nakam mean?"

"Revenge."

"Well, somebody sure got some."

!!☠†☼✴➹☣✖⚡!!

Detective Walsh met with nurse Anna Trebor's supervisor Martha Williams, according to her Anna was an excellent nurse, never had any complaints, she seemed very diligent and caring.

"Did you know if Anna had any friends here at the hospital?" Walsh asked.

"No, none that I know of, she pretty much stayed to herself. I noticed that she never really ate meals with anyone, she was pretty much a lone wolf."

"I see, and she never gave you any reason to suspect that she was an anti-Semitic?"

"No, although now that you mention it we have had a couple of Jewish patients whose diagnoses showed that they should have been routine but developed complications and passed away."

"And these all were patients of Anna Trebor's?"

"I'm afraid so, yes."

"I would like to have copies of those patients records and I recommend that you might want to have them reviewed as well."

"I will speak to the board and I'll have them sent to you tomorrow by courier if that's all right."

"Thank you that will be fine. And thank you again for your time, Mrs. Williams."

Walsh then drove over to Bayer Headquarters near Columbus Circle. He met with several of Otto's coworkers and his immediate supervisor in a conference room that overlooked the Hudson River on the twenty-first floor.

The conclusion was that no one suspected or were ever given any clues that Robert Trebor was an ex-Nazi SS officer. He also was a bit of a loner, never really talked much about his past, some people are like that they said, everyone just thought he was introverted.

His supervisor said he was a good worker, a team player and was a real company man, everyone thought he had a solid future at Bayer, although his lack of sociability would most likely hold him back from making it to the upper echelons of the corporation.

As far as friends, nobody could say that they were any more than an acquaintance, they never got together after work for anything other than an occasional drink, they never were invited to his home and when he attended company functions he only did what was expected.

Walsh was shown Trebor's office, Walsh spent over an hour going thru his desk, his files and notebooks and found nothing that indicated any ties to his past.

Walsh decided to grab some steamed mussels at Carmines on Broadway and W 81st Street. Carmine's is world famous for two things, it's steamed mussels in white wine with garlic and it was the restaurant that Salvador "Porky" Cacciopoli was gunned down in a hail of bullets. Carmine cleaned the place up but never patched the bullet holes in the walls for the tourists. Porky's demise did wonders for Carmine business. Carmine named a dish in honor of Salvador, it's Porky's Neapolitan Pork Rotolini.

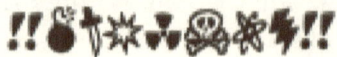

Detective Walsh found Roscoe waiting for him in the lobby of 299 W. 102nd Street.

As Walsh entered the lobby, Roscoe looked at his watch, "Don't tell me, Carmine's."

"I couldn't help it, those mussels are to me as Nathans famous dogs are to you."

"Hey, don't be trying to compare those barnacles to my chili dogs. There's no comparison."

"You're right, there is no comparison."

"Walsh, you're hopeless, come on. I've already gotten the key from the super. It's 8D."

The apartment was furnished in ultra-modern Danish furniture, very simple, very clean lines, lots of dark woods. The place was immaculate, not a hair out of place, it looked more like a showroom than a living room.

Inside the bedroom closet, in a shoe box hidden amongst others they did find photographs of both of them posing proudly wearing their SS uniforms, there were many photographs taken within concentration camps, some of the photos included them, some did not.

There were pictures of graphic images the likes they had never seen before. German soldiers standing proudly posing next to a pile of corpses, stacks of humans so emaciated they looked like skeletons, SS officers standing by bodies being put into ovens, smiling. Photographs of women having their heads shaved so that their hair could be made into work clothes and the linings of the German U-boat crew's boots. One photo showed Anna smiling hold a small table lamp', with the lampshade made of human skin that had the number tattoo from a Jewish inmate.

One thing they all had in common was that they made the Detectives sick to their stomachs knowing that these two would keep such photographs as souvenirs.

Roscoe found a safe-deposit box key from Bank of America taped to the back of a painting. He was anything but an art connoisseur, but he had a feeling that most of these painting were probably stolen artwork taken from the families of wealthy German Jews. He would have the art squad come out the next day and take a look at the paintings to confirm if his suspicions were right.

Roscoe called Captain O'Rourke to give him an update.

"Captain, Roscoe here. They were defiantly Nazis, both were SS officers connected with concentration camps, truly the scum of the earth, I would categorize them both as war criminals.

"Walsh has a lead on the Nakam angle, but it's still too early to draw any conclusions. And we have a safety deposit box we're going to be checking out tomorrow. So, that's where we stand at the moment, we'll know more tomorrow. I'll keep you posted, night Captain."

Walsh and Roscoe were both quiet and contemplative on the ride home. This was going to be a hard case, not so much of the crime but the victims. Usually, you could muster up some sympathy for even the lowest of human beings, criminals, druggies, pimps, even gangster thugs, but Nazis? Roscoe and Walsh had to keep telling themselves it's not about who was killed, it was that they were killed.

Detective Walsh dropped Roscoe off at his house, then went home. Betty had just taken the meatloaf out of the oven when Roscoe walked into the kitchen. Betty could tell something was bothering him, she set the hot pan on the counter and put her arms around his neck and gave him a kiss, "You okay?"

"Yeah, I guess so. This is going to be a hard one, damn Nazis."

"Want to talk about it?"

"Not really, honestly I wish I could forget it. Jimmy and I saw some photographs of our victims, who were involved in unspeakable acts smiling like they were enjoying a day at the beach, I don't think I'll ever be able to get some of those images out of my head."

"You come sit down for dinner."

"Okay, but I'm not very hungry."

"That's okay, you sit down now and I'll bring out a plate for you. And I'll put on the television, I think the Addams Family is on."

"Good, I could use a good laugh."

!!☗†☼⚕☠✖⚡!!

Walsh was waiting in Roscoe's office reading the report from forensics and the medical examiner. Roscoe walked in with two cups of coffee and a half dozen Entenmann's donuts that he picked up from D'Agostinos on his way in.

"Jimmy, what's the good word?"

"Forensics got us a couple good lead's on the rope and the tattoo gun the killers used."

"Great, we'll finish our breakfast and then scope out the led's."

"Breakfast?"

"Shut up and eat your donut, smart ass."

After breakfast, the Detectives drove over to 2626 Mermaid Avenue, Wallinski's Hardware. Wallinski's been around since 1919, it's an old school hardware store, no frills. Their attitude is, you want a shopping experience, go away. If you want hardware, let's talk. Wallinski's small enough to remember what they sell and who they sell it to.

Roscoe and Walsh both have bought all their tools, hardware, plumbing, and electrical supplies from Wallinski. Wallinski is a real mom & pop business, Wally Wallinski has been running the store ever since Roscoe can remember, Wally's grandfather opened the store back in 1919 after he came back wounded from the Great War. He lost an eye when a German grenade blew up in front of him as his outfit was making a charge at the Battle of the Somme. Wally's father, Jerry ran the store for a short time, he passed away at the age of 55 from lung cancer, that's when Wally dropped out of college and took over the store, he's been running the shop for over forty years.

"Hey, Wally my man, what's happening?"

"Hey Roscoe, hey Jimmy, what brings you guys in here, business or pleasure?"

"Business. I guess you probably heard about that incident down in Levy Park?"

"You are kidding, that's all anyone's talking about. Fucking Nazis."

"We think that the rope that was used might have come from here."

"No kidding, well that would be quite an honor, my rope helped hang a couple of dirty stinking Nazis. That would be something."

"Yeah, maybe you could do a whole ad campaign about it."

"You think?"

"Wally, get a grip."

"Sorry, well let me think. Oh yeah, I sold about a hundred feet of rope to a guy in his late thirties, he was about five-ten, dark hair, maybe 175 pounds and he was Jewish."

"How do you know he's Jewish?"

"He was wearing a Yakama, oh and his name was Navan."

"How did you happen to get this name?"

"That's what the girl he was with called him."

"Did you get her name?"

"No, he never said it."

"What did she look like?"

"She was quite thin, maybe five four, short dark hair, she was pretty in a natural way, like a movie star, you know what I mean, not a lot of makeup just a natural beauty. Her eyes."

"What about her eyes?"

"There was a sadness, a look of being lost."

Roscoe nodded knowingly, "Wally, she's probably seen unspeakable abominable murderous acts and has survived such inhuman conditions that would crush even an angel's soul."

Wally gave a faint smile, "My son, Bobby was with the Third Army when they freed Buchenwald, sometimes he gets that same look in his eyes too. I guess there are something's that stay with you for the rest of your life, that you can never speak of because no one would understand."

"It's shitty world out there my friend."

"You know it."

"That I do. Say Wally, just on the off chance that you might know, where would one go to get a tattoo gun?"

"Well, if I don't care about quality, I'd pick it one up at a pawn shop."

"Wally, you're a genius, maybe should become a detective." Walsh said.

"Nah, I couldn't afford the pay cut."

Sneaky Pete's Pawn Shop was a couple of blocks from Nathans Famous on Surf Avenue and 16th Street.

Walsh dropped Roscoe off at Nathans so he could order his usual, Roscoe decided to let Walsh take the lead and deal with Sneaky Pete.

"I'll eat slow, so you come on back after you finish with Mr. Sneaky." Roscoe said as he got out of the car.

Walsh parked the car at Nathans and walked the two blocks to the pawnshop. When he entered there was a man trying to pawn a watch that he claimed was a Rolex that belonged to his father, but when he saw Walsh he decided that he didn't want to hock it after all and almost ran out the door.

"You a cop?" Pete asked Walsh.

"Yeah, you Pete?"

"Sneaky Pete, that's me. What can I do ya for?"

"I'm interested in knowing if you recently sold a tattoo gun?"

"As a matter of fact, I did. It was about four weeks ago, a guy and girl come in asking if I got a tattoo gun and I said yeah, but you don't look like a tattoo artist, whatca ya going to do with it, I said."

"What did he say?"

"He said that he was some kind of artist and was going to an art project with it."

"What did this guy look like?"

"White guy, late thirties, about five-ten, dark hair, maybe 175 pounds and he was Jewish."

"How do you he was Jewish?"

"He was wearing a Star of David around his neck, oh and a Yakama."

"And the girl?"

"She was plain, but pretty like a model, about five-four with short dark hair, She never smiled, which is odd since I'm such a sociable guy, ya know?"

"That is odd. Did you get a name?"

"Name and address, that's the law officer and Sneaky Pete always follows the law."

Walsh got to Nathans before Roscoe had a chance to even finish his second chili cheese dog, he was in mid-bite when Walsh came strolling up, "Navan Renner."

Roscoe mumbled with a mouthful of chili cheese for Walsh to have a seat and slid his partner's lunch towards him.

"Here I got you a chili dog, some fries and lemonade, on me."

"Big spender."

"What?"

"A small fry, you couldn't go for the large fries, thanks."

"Hey, whatta busting my chops for?"

"Fuggedaboutit."

"So, did you get this guy's address, too?"

"1525 Hart Place."

"Hart Place, that's between 15th and 16th Street. Grab your dog and go see if he's there."

"I ain't grabbing nothing, I'm going to sit here and finish this lovely lunch that you were so kind to buy me, then we'll go."

"Geez, Napoleon Solo would have grabbed his dog and gone."

"Roscoe, we're not the "Man from U.N.C.L.E.", you're no Napoleon Solo and I'm not any Illya Nut-cracking!"

"Kuryakin. Illya Kuryakin. Not Nut-cracking."

"Whatever, and don't give me those puppy dog eyes, I'm finishing my lunch and that's all there is to it."

"Fine, be that way."

!! 💣🕇☆🔨💀✳⚡ !!

Navan Renner had just finished packing his bags and was getting ready to call a cab to meet Emme at JFK airport, they were going to immigrate to Israel. The idea that there might be other ex-Nazis walking the streets of New York overwhelmed them both.

Navan thought it best that they go to the airport separately, he worried that the police would soon find out about the rope and tattoo gun and trace it back to him if they did he wanted at least for Emme to get away.

The knock on the door was almost a relief. He placed the phone receiver down and looked at his watch, he had to stall the police at least until Emme's plane took off. He quickly hid his bag in the hallway closet and opened the front door. There were two middle-aged men wearing inexpensive suits, the older of the two was wearing a fedora, something you don't see too often these days. These men were definitely police detectives.

"Yes?"

The man with the hat held up a police badge and stated, "I'm Detective Sergeant Brown and this is my partner Detective Walsh. Are you Navan Renner?"

"Yes I am, what can I do for you Detectives?"

"May we come in?"

"Yes, of course. Please come in."

The inside seemed almost vacant, there was a sofa, one wooden kitchen chair, an orange crate for a coffee table and that was it in the living room, no TV, no lamps just the naked overhead light bulb.

"Please sit down, may I offer you a glass of water? I'm afraid that's all I have to offer."

"No thank you, Mr. Renner. We're investigating the killing of the two people who were found in Levy Park. Would you know anything about that?" Roscoe asked as he and Walsh sat on the sofa.

"Only what I've read in the papers."

"Well, the reason we're asking is that it's come to our attention that you recently purchased a large amount of rope and a tattoo gun."

"Yes, that's right I'm an artist and I needed those for an art project I'm working on."

"Is that right?"

"Yes, I can show you, would you like to see some of my work?"

"If you don't mind?"

"Not at all, please follow me, I work in the basement."

Navan led Roscoe and Walsh down into the basement where there were over a dozen canvases with painted pieces of rope attached to the canvas, along with tattooed arms, legs, and body parts from baby dolls and store mannequins stuck onto the canvasses. The obvious overall theme was Nazis, concentration camps, the Holocaust.

"I'm trying to get enough pieces to have a show, hopefully somewhere in Borough Park. What do you think?"

"Very powerful, Mr. Renner," Walsh said.

"Yes, very powerful." Roscoe agreed. "Mr. Renner, would you mind if I took your tattoo gun back to our lab for analysis?"

"Do you have a warrant?"

"If you're innocent why would you mind?"

"Detective Brown, in 1943 at the age of twenty I was captured and sent to Buchenwald, I worked in the forced labor camps. For two years we worked 12 hours a day, six days a week, we were beaten, whipped and starved, I was one of the fortunate ones who survived. You'll have to excuse me when you say if your innocent what do you have to fear, six million Jews were arrested and murdered, who were innocent, that's what I have to fear."

"You don't really believe that America is the same as Nazi Germany?" Walsh asked.

"No but look at all the innocent colored people in the South that are brutalized and arrested, there have been multiple attacks against innocent Jews and synagogues,

American is a wonderful place don't get me wrong Detective, but you have evil here, too."

"Yes, you're right Mr. Renner, we are not perfect and I understand your position. So, if you require us to get a warrant, that's what we'll do. Detective Walsh will stay with you while I go and obtain a warrant."

"How long will that take?"

"Possibly a couple hours."

Navan looked at his watch, it was two o'clock, their El Al flight nonstop to Tel Aviv was scheduled to depart at four fifteen.

"Fine, go get your warrant."

"Did you have somewhere to be, Mr. Renner? I noticed that you looked at your watch."

"I was going to meet with a couple art galleries."

"I see, well I'll try and be as quick as I can. Oh, before I go what is the name of your lady friend, the one who accompanied you when you purchased the rope and tattoo gun?"

"I'd rather not say."

"Because?"

"This doesn't concern her."

"Jimmy, please keep Mr. Renner company until I return."

"Right."

!! ⚫︎✝︎☆🐾💀✳︎⚡︎!!

Walsh was sitting on the sofa reading the New York Times while Navan sat in the wooden chair opposite the Detective, rocking back and forth with his eyes closed, mumbling a prayer for courage and strength. Walsh wanted to ask him some questions but decided to wait until he finished his praying. After several minutes Navan was silent and opened his eyes.

"Mr. Renner, when Detective Brown returns with the warrant, he will be accompanied by a dozen or so uniformed officers who will perform a complete search of your home, from top to bottom. I just want to alert you to what will happen. Do you understand?"

'What if I decided to give you the tattoo gun now, will you still search my home?"

"I'm afraid so, it's gone too far. Did you want to surrender the tattoo gun?"

Navan looked at his watch again, it was three thirty, Emme was probably in line to board the plane.

"No, not if you're going to search my home anyway. I'll let you find it on your own."

The phone rang, Navan knew it was Emme calling. He was torn whether to answer it or not. Detective Walsh watched him as the phone continued to ring he asked, "Aren't you going to answer it?"

Navan reached over and picked up the receiver.

"Hello? No, I'm sorry but I don't think I can make my appointment. Uh, I have been unexpectedly detained, no you go on ahead with the meeting and I'll try and get there as soon as I can. No, everything is alright, really. I'll call you as soon as I can. Es vet zeyn gleykh, ikh hab dir lib. Zay gezunt."

Navan told her it would alright and that he loved her, but she knew it wouldn't be. Once again she would survive while someone she loved wouldn't. He hung up the phone and looked at Walsh, "My gallery, wondering where I was."

"I hope this won't be too much of an inconvenience, Mr. Renner?"

"It's alright Detective, I've dealt with worse."

There was a knock on the door, Brown and six uniformed officers entered the house, Roscoe handed Navan the search warrant.

"Mr. Renner this is a search warrant authorizing us to search your home."

Navan said nothing, he sat down on the wooden chair and again began to rock in prayer. He stopped when Detective Brown interrupted his prayer, "Mr. Renner, we found this suitcase in the hallway closet, it contains a one-way ticket on a, El Al flight that was scheduled leave today a 4:15."

Nava looked at his watch, smiled and said, "Yes Detective, it appears that I will have to reschedule my flight, as my plans have seemed to have changed."

Police Officer Brad Taylor entered from the basement with the tattoo gun, "I've found the tattoo gun, Detective."

Brown said over his shoulder, "Bag it and get it over to the lab asap. Mr. Renner, would you mind accompanying us to the station?"

"Do I have a choice?"

"Well you could come voluntarily or I can arrest you."

"I'll come voluntarily."

!! ☗†☼♣☠✳✦ !!

"Mr. Renner, your tattoo gun had the blood of Anna and Robert Trebor, would like to explain how that is?" Roscoe asked.

"You're wrong Detective, the blood on the tattoo gun is not that of Anna and Robert Trebor, but of Otto Reittier and Anna Eseese, two known Nazi war criminals."

"Do you admit killing them?"

"I do, they were found guilty in absentia by an Israeli court in 1957 and sentenced to death."

"Are you a representative of the Israeli government?"

"No."

"Mr. Renner this is way beyond my pay grade, this is something the courts are going to have to decide. We're just a couple of simple homicide police trying to solve a murder and it looks like we have. I'm afraid I'm going to have to arrest you, Mr. Renner. Is there anyone you'd like to call, you're entitled to one phone call, maybe a lawyer or someone at the Israeli consulate?"

"Yes, thank you."

Roscoe brought a phone into the interview room and left him alone until he was done. While Navan was on the phone Roscoe sent Walsh to inform Captain O'Rourke that the case was solved and of the particulars.

"Oh man, this is going to be one major league headache. Nazi war criminals an Israeli hit man, why couldn't it have been just some nut-gone apeshit? The DA is going to freak out. Nice job on your end Walsh, convey my congratulations to Roscoe, now I've got to call the commissioner and start the ball rolling."

Roscoe entered the interview room after Navan finished his call with a uniformed officer.

"Mr. Renner, I'm afraid you're under arrest, the officer is going to take you for pictures and fingerprints, then you'll be transferred to Rikers Island. Do you have any questions?"

"No. Detective Brown, I thank you for all your courtesy. I harbor no ill feelings."

"I wish you the best luck, Mr. Renner."

Police Officer Taylor placed handcuffs on Navan and led him downstairs to start to process him into the system.

Roscoe was sitting in his office when Walsh walked in, "Captain sends his congratulations."

"Great, you know this is one time I wouldn't have minded that the killer had gotten away. You know?"

"Hey, like you always say, we just catch the killer and let the system sort it out."

"Do I always say that? I don't remember ever saying that."

"Nope, you always say that."

"Hey, want to grab some dinner?"

"Sure what are you up for?"

"Anything, except German."

The Case of the Graves Creeper

Detective Brown got to his office early, feeling pretty spunky, he and Betty just happen to wake up early and decided to start the day off with a little dancing in the sheets. Normally, afterward they go back to sleep until the alarm clock goes off, but this morning Roscoe was feeling wide-awake. So, while Betty went back to sleep, he got up, showered, shaved, made coffee and toast, left a little love note for Betty and headed down to the 60th Precinct.

He was actually whistling as he walked into the homicide squad room when he ran into his partner Jim Walsh.

"Hey, Jimmy."

"Roscoe, you're not going to believe this, someone killed the groundskeeper at Gravesend Cemetery over on Van Sicklen Street, dug up two women's graves and stole their bodies in the middle of the night."

"Damn you Walsh, you're really bumming me out this morning. And I was feeling gooey."

"Groovy?"

"Aw shut up, let's go."

The ride was only a fifteen-minute drive straight up Shell Road, then three lefts off of Gravesend Neck Road. There were a dozen uniformed officers cordoning off the area from the New York media frenzy, nothing stirs the Big Apple media like murder, especially murder in a graveyard.

English Quakers originally settled Gravesend Bay in 1643, the cemetery was built in 1658 and since then the little cemetery has been neglected and forgotten. It is still in use, but people nowadays are opting for the more deluxe cemeteries like Green-Wood or Holy Cross. Gravesend has very few sites available, most of the people being buried there these days are older established families that had purchased their gravesites decades ago before the neighborhood became less affluent.

Brown and Walsh parked in the alleyway just north of the entrance on Van Sicken and walked to where Officer Levine was holding the hordes of press at bay. As they approached the reporters started to swarm around them peppering them with questions.

"Do you have any leads?"

"Do you know who the victims are?"

"Who could have done such a thing?"

"Is this the act of a lunatic?"

"Do you think it's a satanic cult?"

Roscoe stopped, held up his hand, smiled and said, "No comment, besides we just got here."

He and Walsh ducked under the yellow police tape and headed over to where the ME and crime unit were huddled over the 72-year-old groundskeeper, Dwight Silverberg who had had his throat cut from ear to ear. The ME said that the only thing keeping the old man's head attached to his body was a sliver of skin the width of a shoestring French fry.

Dwight Silverberg had been the groundskeeper at Gravesend for over fifty years. These days there wasn't a lot to do as the groundskeeper, it was more of an administrative job, scheduling the lawn services, maintaining the flower arrangements, on the rare occasion of a burial, coordinating with the gravediggers, the headstone companies and the funeral homes. He never dealt with the families, only the service providers. According to the cemetery owners and his friends, he had no family, he was beloved by everyone who knew him. It looked like old Dwight must have just been at the wrong place at the wrong time, catching the grave robber or robbers in the act and was killed.

The two women whose graves were robbed and bodies were stolen had both been buried within the last eight months.

Roscoe walked over to the coroner who had just finished examining the body of the groundskeeper and asked, "What's your guess on time of death?"

"I'd estimate that the time of death between 2 and 4 a.m."

"Seems like the perfect time to dig up a couple graves. Say Doc, wouldn't the odor from someone who's been dead for eight months be overpowering?" Roscoe asked the coroner.

"It surely wouldn't be a bed of roses or for the faint of heart, or someone with a weak stomach, that's for sure. I'm thinking this guy would definitely have to live in a house or someplace where there aren't any neighbors, I'm guessing somewhere with a basement."

"I would think he probably would need a van or truck to carry two bodies." Walsh surmised.

Roscoe concurred and said, "I agree, say you about done here Doc?"

"Yeah all done, I'll know more once I conduct the autopsy. You'll have my report in the morning, Roscoe."

Walsh signaled for Officer Levine to come over. "Hey Carl, once the crime lab is done here, have some uniforms go door to door and see if anybody saw or heard anything, will ya?"

"Sure thing Detective."

"Thanks."

Walsh rejoined Roscoe over by the two coffins that were laying upended like two beached whales. Roscoe turned to Walsh and asked, "So whatda think?"

"I think we're looking for one sick puppy."

"Yep, I think you're right."

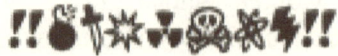

Eddie Grimes became obsessed with his mother after she died, so much so that he wanted to become her. He believed that if he found corpses of women who resembled her he could fashion a woman suit that he could wear and then he would become her and then she would always be with him.

Eddie didn't want to kill the old man, but he came out of nowhere and he shouldn't have tried to stop him. Eddie had just dragged the second coffin out of the grave when he noticed the groundskeeper heading towards him. He stopped prying the top off the second coffin and slipped into the shadows, when the old man got close enough he circled behind him and slit his throat.

Eddie didn't feel bad that he killed the old groundskeeper, he did feel disappointed that it was a man, men weren't useful to him in his quest to construct his mother's suit.

Detective Walsh was right in that the killer did have a van to transport the cadavers. A 1963 Ford Econoline Panel Van, powder blue, with 90,000 miles on the odometer, it's missing the back bumper with minor damage over the right rear tire well, and a broken right rear taillight. Eddie traded his mother's brand new Ford LTD in an even swap for the van in the pre-mentioned condition, which not only surprised the manager of Tommy Fudge Ford and Lincoln but delighted the owner, Tommy Fudge.

When Jerry, the manager came to his boss with the deal, Tommy's first comments was, "Either this guy's a nut or the car is stolen."

Jerry's reply, "Nuts."

Ironically, Eddie thought the folks at Tommy Fudge Ford and Lincoln were nuts.

Eddie Grimes drove into his attached garage at four forty-five in the morning, closed the garage door and began to remove the two corpses from the back of the van. He would carry them down into his basement where he had the others.

The combination of these two just might be what he needed to make the perfect suit that would have made his mother proud. One was the right body type and the other had a good face, the combination of the two that he just might work.

Down in Eddie's basement, there were two chairs covered with human skin, he had also created several human skull bowls that held assorted candies, m&m's, malted milk balls and lifesavers. He had various size lamp shades also covered with human skin, desk lamps, table lamps, and floor lamps.

It was very fortuitous and serendipitous that Eddie's father had been a butcher and owned his own butcher shop in Coney Island, Grimes Prime "A Great Place to Meat."

The basement was the perfect place for Eddie to set up his father's equipment, the stainless steel butchers table, a complete set of hand saws and blades, meat scrapers, bone dust scrapers, boning hooks, liver hooks, meat grinder plates, and an assortment of knives, boning, breaking, cimeter, paring, skinning and fillet. Like most houses in the area, the basement even had a built-in floor drain.

Eddie had worked in his father's butcher shop for over twenty years, he had dreams of taking over the shop someday, unfortunately, Eddie's father, Eddie senior was heavily into betting on the ponies. To cover his debts he borrowed money from a loan shark named Tony "the trigger" Romano, who after Eddie's father failed to repay the loan was the recipient of many a broken bone was found one day burnt to a crisp in Grimes Prime butcher shop.

Two days after his father's death Tony "the trigger" came by the house with his goons to inform Eddie's mother that they expected to be repaid for the loan out of the life insurance money or little Eddie could end up like his father, charbroiled.

After she paid off the loan, she still had enough money to pay off the mortgage of the house and figured she could, if she was frugal have enough for the rest of her life along with her social security.

Life's a funny thing, it never goes how you plan. It seems that on one of the occasions when Tony and his enforcers were busting Eddie senior's balls for missing a payment, Eddie disclosed that he and his wife have been having an incestuous relationship with little Eddie for decades.

Tony sneered, "That's disgusting, you freaking chicken hawk, diddling your own son, that's disgusting! Maybe if you had a really hot daughter I could see it, but your son!"

Tony was so appalled that he had his enforcer whack big Eddie so hard in the testicles that he spent over a month in the hospital. Then two weeks after he was released Eddie was killed in the fire.

Tony Romano, being an entrepreneur and always one to look for an opportunity, called the late Eddie Grimes Senior's widow and informed her that he knew about her little indiscretion with sonny boy and that if she wanted it to stay a secret he would require twenty large to keep his mouth shut.

She hung up the phone, took Eddie to her bedroom and made love to her son, afterward with him sleeping next to her in bed, took the S&W 38 snub nose revolver out from her bedroom nightstand and blew her brains out.

Tony told Eddie Junior that he knew about him fucking his mommy and that it would cost him twenty thousand bucks for Tony to keep his lips sealed. Two months later Tony "the trigger" Romano was found in the kitchen of his favorite Italian Restaurant, Momma Leonarda's hanging on a meat hook gutted, filleted and with his lips cut off his face, sewn together and stuffed up his rectum.

To this day it's an unsolved crime, basically because everyone, even the police couldn't stand "the trigger", so little or no effort was ever put into finding his killer.

For Momma Leonarda it was a blessing, business picked up considerably, as does any restaurant in New York with the prestige of having a mobster killed in or near the premise.

Roscoe and Walsh had the sad task of informing the families of the two women that some ghoul had stolen their loved one's body from their graves.

Mrs. Nina Hollywood of 2333 East 2nd Street, Gravesend had lived and raised six children in the small, modest brick and plank wood, stand-alone, four bedroom house. Nina was a grandmother of eight, her husband Charlie and she had been married for fifty-six years when she passed away at the age of eighty-two from brain cancer. Charlie is currently in the process of selling their home and moving in with his eldest son, James and his family over in Edison, New Jersey.

Mrs. Betty Asbury, a widow living alone at 2282 West 1st Street, Gravesend was killed in her home during a home invasion, Mrs. Asbury was fifty-two when she was murdered. Roscoe and Detective Walsh solved that crime four years ago. Huey Davenport, a crackhead broken in late one night planning on sneaking in, stealing as much as he could carry and the sneak out. Unfortunately for Betty Asbury, Huey was a bit of a klutz and stoned out of his freaking mind when he broke in. After he knocked the Philco color television set off of its stand that woke Mrs. Asbury, he panicked and stabbed her in the heart with a sterling silver carving knife that he later tried to hock, Huey might have gotten away with it, except he forgot to wipe the knife off before trying to pawn it. Huey received life without the possibility of parole.

As they sat in Roscoe's office going over the ME's report and the results from the crime lab, Roscoe finished reading the report from the coroner when he said, "Hey Jimmy, I can't believe that Betty Asbury was one of the women that were snatched, you remember her, she was killed by that druggy Huey Davenport about three or four years ago."

"Yeah, but I haven't found anything that ties these two women together, other than they were buried with months of each other."

"Maybe there isn't any connection other than their graves were in close proximity to each other."

"Just a coincidence?"

"Yeah, just a coincidence. Let's check and see if there have been any other bodies stolen from other cemeteries in the area."

Walsh called the other precincts in Brooklyn and found that there were, in fact, three other incidences of grave robbery, all were women.

Roscoe was sitting like he did when he was trying to think, feet up on his desk, leaning back in his chair with his eyes closed. He sat in silence for over forty minutes before speaking.

"I'm thinking this guy is either a necrophiliac or some kind of Doctor Frankenstein who's collecting different parts to create the ghoul of his dreams."

"Maybe we should talk to a shrink, either way, this is some whacked out shit." Walsh suggested.

"Good Idea, Jim. See if Doc. Reyes was some time to stop by today."

"Will do." Walsh stepped out of Roscoe's office to call the police psychologist from his desk. Walsh had worked with Roscoe long enough to know that when he's kicking back in his chair thinking, it's best to leave him to it.

By time Walsh had talked to Doctor Reyes and arranged for him to swing by in the afternoon, Roscoe was up and moving. Roscoe was wearing his fedora and heading towards Walsh, "Hey Jim, up for a couple of dogs from Nathans?"

"Roscoe, don't you ever get tired of eating hot dogs for lunch every day?

"Walsh, I'll have you know that Nathans chilidogs and fries fill all my nutritional needs in one healthy meal."

"Oh, this is going to be good. How?"

"Well, you got your meat which is your protein, you got your beans for carbohydrates, you got your cheese for your vitamin D, C, and B12, you got the bun which is your fiber and finally you got your French fries for your potassium. So, you want to grab a dog?"

Walsh stood there stunned with his mouth open in amazement, "Okay, sure."

"You know Walsh sometimes you surprise me.

!! 🕯️✝☆🔱💀✳⚡ !!

Doctor Reyes had been the Brooklyn Police Department's psychologist for eleven years and never had been called to give assistance with the six 0. He had on rare occasions met with a couple of the officers who had been involved in a shooting, either shooting someone or being shot themselves, but never in an advisory role in helping to solve a crime.

"So, Detectives Brown and Walsh how might I help you?"

"Well Doc, we need help. We have a murder that involves grave robbing, and by that, I mean the abduction of corpses, women corpses. So far there have been a total of five, coffins dug up and bodies stolen.

"The two theories that I've come up with are either this guy is a necrophiliac or he's some kind of Doctor Frankenstein."

"All valid theories Roscoe, there are a couple of other possibilities, I've also heard that body snatchers will steal bodies for black magic, for exporting human skeletons for medical purposes, and then there's trying to collect a ransom from the family."

"So far none of the families have been contacted about a ransom, so I think we can eliminate kidnapping." Walsh said.

Doctor Ryes took out his pipe; he then went thru the ritual of meticulously loading the tobacco into the pipe bowl, tamping the tobacco down, inspecting it and then finally lighting the bowl, he took a couple of puffs, inspected the job that he had just done, before speaking again.

"Detectives, it is my professional opinion that you are looking for a man who is, as you stated earlier is a kind of Doctor Frankenstein. I've ruled out him being a necrophiliac, primarily because they usually tend to keep one body for months before using another. No, I think this man is using these women to construct or assemble some sort of creature."

"Any idea where we should start looking, Doc?" Asked Roscoe.

"Well, I would imagine he has recently lost an important female figure in his life, like a mother or wife. My bet would be a domineering mother."

"But why multiple women Doc, why not look for one who just resembled his mother, or better yet, why not just dig up the original mother?" Walsh asked.

"Who knows, maybe the mother was cremated, or the body so mangled, or died overseas or even out at sea, who knows."

"Okay thanks, Doctor Reyes, we'll start checking out the obituaries, cross-checking to see who have surviving sons, who have access to vans or trucks and live in a stand-alone home." Roscoe said.

Walsh added, "Now the fun begins."

Seventy-four year old Nina Hollywood lay naked on Eddies Grimes butcher's table, the smell was so horrendous Eddie wore an activated charcoal face mask with an air purifier, two Ozone Generators and six buckets of baking soda placed around the basement to help combat the stench.

Eddie selected a ten-inch fillet carving knife and began, he started at the groin on the right side, and he slipped the knife blade point under the skin and slowly worked his way upwards to the neck, he then repeated the process on the left side.

Once he had completed slicing the complete torso, he began to roll the skin off Mrs. Hollywood, careful not to rip or tear the skin around the breasts. He carefully carried the prize over to a wooden table that was covered with baby powder and laid it out flat. He stood looking proudly at his handy work, the first three women were basically practice runs, although there were some parts from his first attempts that he could use in case he needed them.

He flipped Nina over onto her stomach and began to fillet her back, from the base of her neck to the top of her knees; the hardest part was going to be not destroying the buttocks. He had had problems with skinning the first three with tearing or ripping especially when he worked around the anus, but for some reason, Nina was being very cooperative.

After he has successfully removed the back skin and placed next to the front piece, he delicately turned her onto her back, tied her legs so they were positioned up into the air, removed his pants and mounted her. As he was having intercourse with Nina Hollywood, he thanked her for being so obliging, not like those others, she was special. Maybe he would keep her.

He carefully untied her legs, picked her up and carried her to the walk-in freezer in the corner of the basement. He laid her gently down on the ground, not hanging up on a meat hook like the others. He kissed her on the lips and whispered how special she was. He closed the door and turned off the light inside the freezer.

Eddie picked up the two pieces of skin that were lying on the wooden table and carried them over to the table where a sewing machine was, he sat down and began to sew the front and back pieces together on his mother's Singer industrial sewing machine, he would stop from time to time to try the "suit" on. Every time he did he would stand up in front of a full-length mirror he had leaning against the wall. When he did, he felt a special connection to his dead mother, soon he would become his mother.

"I got six possible, how about you Jimmy?"

"I got five."

"Eleven, that's not too bad. Where do you want to start?"

"How about with Mr. Don Meyers at 198 Bay 41st Street?"

"Okay, Mr. Meyers it is."

Walsh went down to the K-9 Squad and picked up Bonzo, a German Shepherd with a nose for the dead. Bonzo was the best cadaver dog in all of Brooklyn, he could find, locate, detect, expose, uncover, reveal, and uncover the dearly departed. Bonzo could sense if someone had had even the slightest contact with the dead. When he detected anything cadaverous, he went crazy, barking, scratching bouncing up and down, hence the name Bonzo.

By six p.m. they had interviewed eight of the eleven prospected suspects, but so far they all seemed rather normal, whatever that means these days and they all passed the Bonzo test.

"Let's call it a day and hit it bright and early tomorrow, what do ya say?" Roscoe asked.

"Sounds like a plan. Let's see, tomorrow we'll start off with Mr. Eddie Grimes over on Mill Road. It says his mother committed suicide about a year ago and get this his father was suspected of having been murdered by Tony "the trigger" Romano."

"Oh boy, can't wait. This guy's got to be a total whack job."

By the time Walsh drove Roscoe home, it was close to seven, Roscoe and Bonzo got out of the car. Roscoe leaned into the passenger window and asked, "Hey, want to come up for dinner? Betty won't mind."

"Thank you, but no. I'm meeting Officer Miller for dinner."

"Miller? Isn't she the tall blond with the legs that won't quit, working Bunko?"

"Yeah, she's the one."

"She's nice if you know what I mean and I think you do."

"Good night Roscoe."

"Hey, I'm just saying."

"I know what you're saying. Go away."

"Okay, but…"

"Go!"

Betty greeted Roscoe and Bonzo when they walked into the apartment, Roscoe got a hot kiss and a cold beer, and Bonzo got a nice ear rub. Bonzo and their cat Lucifer, the saber-tooth kitty that they had adopted got along fine after Bonzo tried to sniff the cat's butt and she whacked him on the nose.

Betty didn't feel like cooking so they ordered a pizza delivered and the turned the television to WPIX to watch the Yankees, even though they stunk that year, 25 games behind Minnesota, disgraceful.

As they sat snuggled up next to each other wearing their Yankee hats on the sofa and watching the game, Bonzo lay at the foot of the sofa and slept while Lucifer slept next to Betty on the couch. Roscoe told Betty a little bit of the case, not too much because as creepy as it was, he had a hunch it was going to get a whole lot creepier.

The game went into extra innings, by the thirteenth inning both Roscoe and Betty were fast asleep, around three thirty Roscoe woke up to Alfred Hitchcock's Psycho on television, Vera Miles was going down the stairs to discover Anthony Perkin's mummified mother in the basement. He thought as scary as that movie was, he had a bad feeling that Psycho would have nothing on this case. And he was right.

When Walsh pulled up to Roscoe's apartment building, he found Roscoe and Bonzo waiting patiently outside watching all the passerby's, occasionally someone would stop and admire Bonzo. If it was a man, Roscoe would tell them he was a working police dog and wasn't allowed to fraternize with John Q Public, however, if it was a cute young lady wanting to adore Bonzo, he was available for pets and hugs, Bonzo not Roscoe.

By the time they arrived at the Grimes residence, it was nine o'clock. They no sooner got out of the car when Bonzo started acting up, the closer they got to 2663 Mill Road the more Bonzo reacted.

"I think we may have a winner." Roscoe stated

"Think I should call for backup?"

"Oh yeah, I think that might be a really good idea"

Detectives Walsh and Brown walked around the small one-story bungalow, unlike the other homes on the block 2663 stood alone, it wasn't an attached home, it was a single dwelling, surrounded by a nice well-kept yard with a white plastic picket fence. Roscoe figured that the house was a holdover from the twenties, it was the type of homes that originally made up this neighborhood, before the real estate developers and landlords figured out that they could double, triple or even quadruple their profits by getting rid of yards and attaching the homes side by side or building three or four-story apartment buildings. 2663 was an oasis of a time gone by in the middle of America's new crowed suburbia.

They noticed that all the windows of the house were blacked out and there appeared to be some freshly turned dirt in the side yard. The two detectives were pretty sure that Mr. Eddie Grimes was their man.

Three black and whites pulled up to where Roscoe and Walsh were waiting, Walsh gestured for them to disperse and then the six officers surrounded the house. Roscoe went to the front door with Detective Walsh standing behind him holding the canine and knocked on the door.

The door slowly opened, nothing in all their years on the NYPD could have prepared them for what they were about to see. Standing before them was a man wearing a suit of human skin that was crudely stitched together, a human skin facial mask, where his eyes and mouth peered thru the holes that were cut out from the face of Betty Asbury, he had scalped Betty and was wearing her hair as a wig. Eddie had no clothes on under the suit of skin, Roscoe and Walsh were staring at what was once Nina Hollywood's nude body.

"May I help you?" Eddie said in a higher voice than was normally his.

Both Roscoe and Walsh were standing like deer in the headlights, the only thing that snapped them back to life was Bonzo barking and going berserk.

"I'm Detective Brown and this is my partner Detective Walsh." He said as he held up his badge.

"You'll have to excuse me, Detectives, you caught me before I had a chance to get dressed. Won't you come in?"

"And who am I addressing, Ma'am?"

"Oh I'm sorry, I'm Mrs. Grimes. Will you give me a few moments to get dressed?"

"Yes Ma'am, we'll wait for you if that's all right?"

"Please make yourself comfortable, I'll be right back."

Once Eddie left the room, Roscoe had Walsh call Doctor Reyes and had him get over there asap, while he went down to investigate the basement.

Eddie Grimes never did stand trial, he was declared mentally insane, and was admitted to Matteawan State Hospital for the Criminally Insane for the remainder of his life.

Detectives Brown and Walsh, along with Doctor Reyes received numerous commendations for their work in the capture of such a menace to society from the police commissioner and the Mayor.

To celebrate, Roscoe decided to treat the three of them to lunch at Nathans. Afterward, as they were walking on the boardwalk, Roscoe asked, "Hey Doc. do you know what a Freudian slip is?"

"Yes I do, do you?"

"Yeah, it's when you say one thing but mean your mother. Pretty funny, huh Doc?"

"Pretty funny, Roscoe."

The Case of the Glass Slipper

"You have the right to remain silent. Anything you say can and will be used against you in a court of law. You have the right to have an attorney. If you cannot afford an attorney, one will be provided for you. Do you understand these rights as I have read to you?" Roscoe stated.

"Yeah, I want my lawyer."

"Fine this interview is over, you're going to be arrested and sent over to Rikers Island. You know that you're the first person I've read those rights to?"

"Ew, lucky me."

1966 was the first year that the police were required to read suspects their Miranda Rights. Most cops didn't like it, they felt it gave the bad guys the edge. In the old days, the police could lean on a suspect to persuade them to confess or at least jog their memories, but those days were over.

Trent Rodriguez had zero respect for women, ever since his mother allowed his father to physically and verbally abuse them, the daily beatings, the constant belittlement, and the total neglect starting at the age of six.

His father was a day laborer, everyday rain or shine, snow or sleet he would stand out on street corners at construction sites with others waiting for construction foremen who needed extra help would cruise by in their pickup trucks and point to those he felt was worthy to work. Often they would have to pay the foreman to pick them to let them work. There was never any health care, or taxes taken out, never a paycheck, it was always strictly cash for a day's labor.

Trent's father would slap him and his mother around when they ever got sick and they had to buy drugs, which was money that could have gone to buy his Old Crow Whiskey.

"You little shit, you're always sick. You're costing me too much money, it's your mother's fault you're always sick, she doesn't take care of you. Maybe I should just let you die."

Trent took the beating and abuse until one day when he was fifteen, his drunken father started to beat his mother, Trent went into his bedroom and picked up a Louisville Slugger and knocked him out with the baseball bat, fracturing his skull. Trent packed what few belongings he had and left home and joined the Crazy Homicides, a notorious Coney Island street gang.

They specialized in extortion, stickups, robbery, dealing dope and they weren't averse to murder. Trent moved right on up in the organization after he was arrested for the murder of Sally Price, a waitress that he kidnapped. He took her to the gang's "clubhouse", raped her and brutally beat her to death while she was bound to a glass table and left her there, where the police found her body still bound to the coffee table.

The arresting officers decided not to bother reading Trent his Miranda Rights, nor did the Detectives that headed up the case, they did obtain a confession with some prompting with a Brooklyn phone book that they slammed upside his head numerous times. Because he was denied his rights subsequently Trent's confession was thrown out of court and he was let go.

Captain O'Rourke called on Roscoe and Walsh to try and salvage the bungled investigation.

"I want you two to see if there's anything that you can do to nail this scumbag. I can't believe that Ehrlich and Chandler fucked this up royally, they knew better than not to read this punks his rights. See what you can do." He said as he handed Roscoe the file on the Price murder.

"We'll give it a shot, Captain."

"Thanks Roscoe, keep me up to date."

"Will do."

As they were heading back to Roscoe's office Walsh said, "I know a couple guys in the gang unit, let's go have a chat."

"Sounds good."

They went downstairs into the basement where the gang unit was tucked away out of site. The unit had its own entrance, so they could come and go as needed. Some of the cops had infiltrated a couple of the gangs, so they had to be clandestine in there showing up to the precinct. Most of the time they would be arrested and brought in as a cover, but occasionally they had to sneak in on their own.

The two gang members that Detective Walsh knew were going by the names Bumpy and Gunner, and while they were undercover that's all they would answer to. Gunner was in the Crazy Homicides while Bumpy was a member of the Rubble Kings.

Gunner knew Trent by his gang name, Spyder. After the screw up he went around boasting how he got away with murder.

"Yeah, he's a piece of work. The kind of guy who likes to pull the wings off of birds."

"Don't ya mean flies?" Roscoe asked.

"No, I mean birds. He's a real freakazoid."

"If you could nose around and see if there's anything you might be able to find out that we could use." Walsh urged.

"Sure, I'll see what I can find out."

Over the next three months, there had been several raids by the gang unit on the Crazy Homicides as well as the other local gangs. There were the usual arrests for harassing citizens on the boardwalk, a couple drive-bys, although if it was gang on gang violence and no civilians were involved, the boys in the gang unit really didn't give a crap. Their thought was just let the creeps kill each other off, Coney Island would finally be rid of them.

Not that anyone could prove it, but it had been rumored that the cops would from time to time leak to a rival gang, something the Crazy Homicides was guilty of against the other gang in hopes that major rumble would happen and there would be no survivors.

Walsh and Roscoe were going over the crime lab reports for the umpteenth time when Roscoe noticed something odd, he found two pages that had been stuck together all this time. It was a statement from one of the women in the Lady Homicides, the women's gang that were at times independent from C.H. Her street name was Angel Eyes, she told police that at the time of the murder she and Spyder were lovers and that he caught her and Sally in bed together and he went crazy. Spyder beat her so badly that she was hospitalized, although she told the doctors that she had been in a motorcycle accident, while she was in the hospital Spyder took his revenge out on Sally, he later told Angel Eyes that he raped Sally and beat her to death, he swore that if she ever told anyone he would kill her too.

Roscoe and Walsh went to have a talk with Detectives Ray Ehrlich and Tony Chandler about the statement of Angel Eyes. Neither one of them had an office, they had desks in the squad room with the other detectives, only Detective Sergeants had offices.

Raymond Ehrlich and Tony Chandler been with the 60th Precinct for twenty-eight years and with homicide for twelve. Both he and his partner Tony were old school cops who believe that Miranda Rights are for pussies. The only rights they believe that punks, thugs, and degenerates deserve is a swift knee to the nuts.

Ray and Tony were clearly annoyed that their case was being taken over by these two goody two shoes.

"So, Ray what can you tell us about this Angel Eyes?" Roscoe inquired.

"Like what?"

Roscoe wasn't in the mood to be taking crap from these two screw-ups. He leaned down and got nose to nose with Ehrlich.

"Hey, listen to me you lazy sack of shit, this isn't the first time Walsh and I had to come in and clean up you guy's mess, so don't be giving me any attitude, understand? Well, do you?" He shouted.

Time stood still and the entire squad room got so quiet you could hear Roscoe's Timex watch tick. Ray straightened up in his chair and answered, "Angel Eyes, her name is Jenny Jones, as far as we know she's drop out of sight, we can't find her. The DA offered her protection, but she refused, so the case went nowhere after we forgot to read him his rights."

"Forgot? Yeah right. Come on Walsh let's go."

The other detectives in the squad room gave Roscoe a wide berth, he rarely blows up, but when he did everyone knew to duck for cover.

Walsh and Roscoe pulled up to a small abandoned warehouse on Surf Avenue that was currently occupied by the Crazy Homicides. Next to the structure was an empty lot where a dozen or so motorcycles were parked.

He and Walsh got out of the car and headed to the warehouse, Roscoe was putting on his fedora when two twenty-something men wearing the CH biker style jackets walked by and one made the quip, "Hey, it's Joe Friday."

Still angered by his exchange with Ehrlich Roscoe's retort was, "Hey, its shit for brains."

The one who made the remark stopped, "You think you're funny?"

Roscoe ignored him and continued to walk to the warehouse.

"Yeah, you better keep walking old man, I'll kick your ass."

Roscoe stopped and turned around, "Bring it on punk."

A crowd of gang members started to come out of the doorway and form a circle around Roscoe and Walsh. They began to jeer and encourage the young tuff to take on the old man.

Roscoe handed his hat to Walsh, who took it and moved to one side. The punk made a charge towards Roscoe, who took a sidestep and tripped his would-be assailant sending him hard down to the pavement. The crowd was shouting and cheering for him to get up, he slowly got up onto one knee, then sprang upwards and tried to tackle Roscoe. Roscoe had anticipated the move and as the boy was in mid-air Roscoe brought his right knee up to meet the charging boy's chin, knocking him unconscious.

Roscoe took his hat back from Walsh, stylishly put it on and headed towards the door, the crowd parted like the Red Sea for Moses leaving the gang members standing in awe of the old man in the hat. They then began beating on the boy for losing, teaching him a lesson and humiliating him even more.

Roscoe and Walsh went into the warehouse and found an older gang member lying around on an old torn up couch with his feet propped up on a glass table that was identical like the one Sally Price was raped and killed on.

"Who are you?" Roscoe inquired.

"Hondo"

"You weren't interested in the fight outside?" Walsh asked.

"Didn't need to see Poncho get his ass kick by un viejo policia."

"Hey, I'm not that old." Roscoe replied.

Once he knew that Roscoe understood Spanish he asked, "Qué deseas?"

"I want to talk to Trent Rodriguez."

"Quien?"

"Spyder."

"Ah, Spyder."

"Is he here?"

"He's not here?"

"No."

"Do you know where we could find him?"

"Probably at his home.

"And that would be where?"

"One one two Mackenzie Street, he and his old lady are renting the stand-alone garage."

"Who's his girlfriend?

"Angel Eyes."

"Gracias."

They walked out on to the street, the crowd was gone, the punk was gone, but when they reached their car, the right front tire had been slashed.

Walsh smiled and said, "Want I should call Triple A?"

"Very funny, I'll get the jack."

!! ⚫†✵⚓💀✳⚡!!

One house in from the corner sat a free-standing one car garage with a Harley Davidson motorcycle parked outside, around on the right side was a door.

Walsh knocked several times, they heard a dog barking from inside, finally, a small woman who they recognized to be Jenny Jones answered the door. She looked to have been asleep, her hair was all a mess, no makeup, bruises on her arms and a hint of a black eye, wearing a man's tee shirt and a pair of pink panties stood in the doorway, "Yeah?"

"I'm Detective Brown and this is my partner Detective Walsh, we'd like to speak to Trent Rodriguez."

"He isn't here."

"Can we come in?"

"You got a warrant?"

"Do we need one? We just want to talk, we're not narcs and unless you got a large stash of coke sitting around in there, we don't care."

"Okay but leave the door open."

As they entered, the dog that was a small brown Heinz 57 mixed breed, stayed close to its master.

"What's the dog's name?" Walsh asked.

"Bandit."

The place was a pig sty, There was an open sofa bed with the sheet and blanket all jumbled up, a glass coffee table next to the sofa bed with looked to be a small baggie of marijuana and other drug paraphernalia, a small card table with a pile of empty beer cans and dirty plates stacked up. Two mismatching wooden chairs tucked under the table and piles and piles of clothes lying all around the floor of the garage. Walsh and Roscoe sat on the two wooden chairs, Jenny sat cross-legged on the sofa bed.

Roscoe took off his hat, "Do you know where Trent is?"

"You think he tells me? He tells the dog more than me."

"Why do you stay with him, he beats you up, he treats you like crap and he's a murderer?"

"Whadda ya want?"

"We're investigating the murder of Sally Price."

"I don't know nothing."

"That's not what you told the Detectives before."

"I don't know nothing."

"She don't know nothing." Trent said as he walked into the garage. He snapped his fingers at Jenny, "Get me a beer."

Jenny jumped off the sofa bed and walked to the tiny refrigerator filled with nothing but beer and brought him one, she then plopped back down on the mattress.

"Whadda ya pigs want?"

"We're investigating the rape and murder of Sally Price."

"Never heard of her."

"No? You were convicted of her murder."

"Didn't you hear, it wasn't me, I was acquitted?"

"No, not acquitted, found guilty, but you lucked out because of a couple of lazy cops you beat the system."

"Yeah, that's me Mr. Lucky."

"Well, just so you know Mr. Lucky, me and my partner here, we're not lazy. Sooner or later you're going to screw up and we'll be there."

"Ew, I'm shaking in my boots."

Roscoe stood up replaced his fedora and proceeded to leave, he stopped next to Trent, "Yeah, you think you're one tough hombre, raping young girls and beating them up, but you're nothing but a punk. Listen, you ever feel like taking on someone other than little girl's tough guy, here's my card. I'm a lot older than you, so it will be a fair fight. Anytime, anywhere punk."

Walsh and Roscoe headed to the evidence room to re-exam all the physical evidence collected at the crime scene, the glass coffee table, the rope that he tied her up with and all her clothes. They compared the original crime photographs with what they were physically looking at with magnifying glasses.

"Hey Roscoe, take a look at this."

"Whadda ya got?"

While Walsh was examining the glass coffee table, he noticed looking down from above of the table that the top was covered with a lot of blood smears and blood splatter and even along the edges of the table, but when he turned the table over there was what appeared to be a blood-soaked fingerprint that was obscured from all the blood on top of the glass.

"I think this might be a fingerprint that wasn't documented. It definitely was left there at the time of the murder."

Roscoe viewed it with his magnifying glass and said, "Nice work Jimmy, let's get a dactylographer down here."

"You mean someone from latent prints?"

"So sue me, I'm just trying to class the joint up, okay?"

Officer Jan Dobris from Latent Prints came over from the crime lab and took several photos, dusted and lifted the print. She held the impression up to the light, "It's a good clean print, give me a couple hours to try and see if we can get a match."

"Great, thanks Jan." Roscoe said.

"Hey Jan, what is your title?" Walsh asked as she was packing up her gear.

"I'm a dactylographer, why?"

"Just wondered, thanks."

Roscoe crossed his arms and smirked.

"Shut up!"

!! 💀†☆⚓☠✴⚡!!

"Trent Rodriguez, you have the right to remain silent. Anything you say can and will be used against you in a court of law. You have the right to have an attorney. If you cannot afford an attorney, one will be provided for you. Do you understand these rights as I have read to you?" Roscoe stated.

"Yeah, I want my lawyer."

Roscoe, Walsh and a half a dozen uniforms officers captured him sleeping at his garage/house at three thirty in the morning, he was totally wasted and wasn't truly coherent until after seven a.m. Jenny was in bed with him, she wasn't arrested although she was brought down to the station for questioning. She indicated that she might be willing to testify but was scared of reprisals from the Crazy Homicides.

"If you cooperate, we can protect you." Roscoe promised.

"With this new evidence, he will be gone for a long, long time." Walsh added.

She said she had to think it over, so Jenny was released.

Trent Rodriguez was booked, had pictures and prints taken and then sent down to the tombs at Rikers Island to be held until a hearing was scheduled to set bail, if he was eligible, which nobody thought he would be. Bail was denied, but due to a mix up with another inmate named Trent

Rodriguez, Trent Rodriguez aka Spyder was able to obtain bail and was now out on the streets.

Roscoe was enjoying a nice dinner at home with Betty and their next-door neighbors, Doctor David, and Laurie Shapiro when his partner Jimmy Walsh called to break the bad news. Betty answered the call, "Oh, Hi Jimmy. Roscoe? Yeah, he's here. Okay, hang on a minute and I'll get him."

She placed the receiver down next to the phone and shouted, "Roscoe, it's for you. It's Jimmy."

"Hey, Jimmy what's the good word?"

"You're not going to believe this."

"Don't tell me, you're going to spoil my dinner, aren't you?"

"Fraid so, Rodriguez was accidentally given bail. He's out."

"How long ago?"

"A couple hours."

"We got to get a patrol car over to that dumpy little garage he and Jenny are staying at."

"I did that already, and I've put out an APB on him. Hopefully, we'll nab him before too long."

"Well, that's all we can do at the moment. Keep me posted."

"Will do."

"Night, and thanks."

He hung up the phone and went back into the dining room, all attention was drawn to him.

"That was my partner, we had a prisoner accidentally get mixed up with another inmate and was he was released on bail, so now we have to find him all over again."

"What's he done?" Laurie asked.

"He raped and killed a young woman. Ah, but this isn't the kind of dinner talk we should be having. Hey Doc., can you believe those Yankees, 25 games out of first."

For the next couple of weeks, Trent Rodriguez was nowhere to be found. The patrol cars kept an eye on his garage/house and the Crazy Homicide's clubhouse. They check all known previous addresses, but nothing.

It took Roscoe and Walsh a long time to track down his parents, who due to Trent's father's drinking problem and not being able to keep a steady job had eventually become homeless.

They moved from one shelter to another, until his mother, Maria couldn't take the beatings and abusive behavior anymore and left him. She turned to prostitution, lived in a flophouse hotel, the Mayfair Arms down on 101st Street on the edge of Bay Ridge, just a couple blocks from the Verrazzano-Narrows Bridge. Neither of his parents had seen or heard from Trent in over six years.

Jenny had either gone underground, ran off with Trent or he killed her, either way, she wasn't around. They contacted her known friends and family, but to no avail.

Trent's court date was approaching, Roscoe contacted his public defender, Charles Wattes to see if he knew where Trent was or at least had heard from him. But, Wattes was completely in the dark, his client was starting to face a number of additional charges on top of his murder charge.

Wattes told Roscoe that he did have one name that he found while going over his notes that he felt wasn't going to cross the attorney-client privilege, Scott Ackley.

Trent met Scott while in Rikers, they were cellmates, Trent had mentioned him to be really dumb witted, mentally slow and pliable, the kind of guy who the other cons could take advantage of, an easy mark. He had been beaten up a couple of times and stabbed once because someone wanted his blanket.

Trent convinced him that they were pals, but Trent was just taking advantage of him as well. Scott was so desperate to make a friend he would do whatever Trent asked him to do.

Roscoe and Walsh went to see Scott Ackley in Rikers, the warden had moved him into the isolation ward for his own safety.

"I want to thank you for taking the time to meet with us Scott, how are you doing?" Roscoe said.

"I'm much better now that I'm away from the other prisoners, they were mean to me. Please call me Scotty, people I like, I like to have them call me Scotty. And I like you."

"Thank you, I like you, too. Why are you in here, Scotty?"

"Me and my friend tried to steal some money from a supermarket, but a man got hurt."

"Did you hurt him, Scott?"

"No, my friend did, he had a gun and shot the nice man. He hurt the man really bad. It's Scotty, please"

"Scotty do remember a man named Trent Rodriguez, he was your cellmate?"

"Yeah, I liked Trent a lot, he was nice to me. He was my friend. He called me Scotty, too. We would do nice things for each other."

"Like what?"

"He would keep the mean prisoners from hurting me when my mother would send me things I would share with him. And when he got out he called me and asked me how I was doing."

"That is nice, he must care for you a lot."

"Yeah, and he said that they would look in on my mother to make sure she was doing fine."

"Where does your mother live Scotty? Maybe we can look in on her too."

"That would be very nice of you. She lives in Williamsburg at 75 Penn Street on the second floor, apartment 2B. When you see her would you tell her I'm fine and that I love her and I'll be home soon."

"Okay Scotty, we will, you take care of yourself."

"Oh, and if you see Trent, tell him "Hi" for me and that I hope I'll see him soon."

"You know Scotty, I have a feeling that you just might."

!! ☗†✡✦☠✲⚡!!

On the way to Williamsburg to check on Mrs. Ackley, Roscoe called for backup. No sirens, no lights and for the responding officers to sit tight until the Detectives arrive.

They pulled up to find four black and whites parked on either side of the building waiting for them. When Roscoe and Walsh got out of their car so did the police officers, they were carrying shotguns and had pistols drawn, one had a battering ram.

Walsh showed the officers Trent's picture and said, "He might be armed and he's already killed once, so be careful." Walsh directed two officers to go around to the back, while he and Roscoe took two with them and left two downstairs in the lobby.

The building was a three story walk up, no elevator with two apartments on each floor. They climbed the stairs up to the second floor, opened the stairwell door and quietly approached the door for 2B. They all strained to see if any of them could hear and sounds coming from inside, nothing.

The two armed police officers stood to either side of the doorway with shotguns at the ready. Roscoe knocked on the door and announced, "Mrs. Ackley, this is the police, please open the door."

There was no sound, Roscoe knocked again, "Mrs. Ackley, this is the police, please open the door."

Finally, they heard someone open the peephole and heard a man's voice, "Hey pig, if you try to come in, I'll off the old lady."

Roscoe responded, "I want to hear Mrs. Ackley say that she's alright."

"She's fine."

"I need to hear it from her."

"Okay, don't try anything or I'll kill her."

Roscoe had Walsh move away from the door and signaled for the officer with the battering ram to get ready.

"Trent, this is Detective Brown, I need to hear from Mrs. Ackley to make sure she's alright."

Roscoe heard the sound of Trent inside running around the apartment, opening windows looking outside to see if there were more police and if he could make a break for it.

"Trent, I need to hear from her, now."

They then heard a sad attempt from Trent to disguise his voice to try and be that of a woman, "Hello, I'm fine officers, please go away."

Roscoe gave a nod and the officer with the battering ram swung around with all his might and splintering the door handle with such force that it propelled the door open knocking Trent who was standing behind it backward.

They observed Trent stumbling backward in what looked to be slow motion, with his arms flailing madly in the air trying to gain control but tripping on his own feet, he ended up crashing awkwardly onto Mrs. Ackley's brand new modern walnut and glass coffee table that she recently purchased from Bloomingdales.

Trent landed headlong onto the table shattering the glass top. Because Mrs. Ackley couldn't afford the extra thick half-inch glass top that was made with tempered glass, she opted for the quarter inch non-tempered glass that has a tendency to shatter, which is what it did. Unfortunately for Trent when the glass top shattered several shards of glass cut ended up slicing the main artery in his neck.

Roscoe tried to stop the bleeding, but without success. By the time the paramedics reach Mrs. Ackley's apartment Trent had bled out, all 5.5 litters, he looked as white as Casper the ghost. They found Mrs. Ackley's body in the bedroom, she had recently beaten to death. It looked like Trent had collected everything he could pawn in a small suitcase and was getting ready to leave when they foiled his plans.

!! 🕯️✝️✴️🔻💀✴️⚡!!

Later that day when they made their report to Captain O'Rourke on all that had happened, they learned that the body of Jenny "Angel Eye" Jones had been found in the garage/house beaten to death and her dog Bandit stabbed to death.

"You know Captain, it's ironic that Trent was killed on a glass table and I guess there's some poetic justice in it, too." Roscoe mused.

"You know Roscoe, I feel bad for Scott Ackley, he was just trying to help someone who he thought was his friend and it resulted in his mother being killed." Walsh said.

"Well Jimmy, it's like you always say, No good deed goes unpunished."

"I don't always say that you do."

"I do, really? Oh okay, well, wanna grab a couple dogs at Nathans?"

"Now that's something you do always say."

O'Rourke said, "Yeah always. By the way Roscoe, if you're going bring me back a chilidog."

As the two detectives were leaving O'Rourke's office, Roscoe turned to Walsh and said under his breath, "He always says that."

M. Ward Leon

The Case of A Brush With Death

Mrs. Beazley was a stay at home mother of two, Tommy age 8 and Wendy age 12. Mr. Beazley worked as a baker at the New York Bread Company on Neptune Avenue in Coney Island. They had managed to purchase a modest home on West 27th Street, just off of Mermaid Avenue, conveniently located near the bakery and P.S. two eighty-eight where Tommy and Wendy both went to school. Marge and Barry Beazley were high school sweethearts and gotten married a couple years later after Barry did a stint in the Navy as a cook. Marge was a natural redhead with a million freckles, which Barry loved. she was a couple inches taller than Barry, she wore her hair down to her shoulders and if a strong wind blew Barry said it might just blow her away.

Marge filled her days with ironing, grocery shopping, cleaning and of course cooking. Once a week, usually on Tuesdays, her and the neighbor ladies would get together for a rousing game of Mahjong, they would alternate homes so everyone would have the chance to act as hostess.

One beautiful spring day Marge was doing some ironing for the kids, she always had the kid's school clothes ironed, so they would look neat, fresh and tidy. There was a ring of the doorbell.

She peered out the peephole to see a well-dressed man in a coat and tie, Marge opened the door. There stood a well-groomed, smiling gentleman who said, "Good morning, I'm your Fuller Brush Man, and I have a gift for you. May I step in a for a moment?"

"Of course, please come in." Marge said as she opened the door all the way. Who wouldn't want a free gift from the Fuller Brush Man?

The man bent down and scooped up his sample case and walked into the living room, sat down and opened up his case and presented Mrs. Beazley with a complimentary toilet brush.

"Take a look at these bristles, Madam. Wouldn't you agree that these are unlike anything that you've ever seen before in a toilet brush? We at Fuller Brush pride ourselves that our brushes are uniquely designed to give you maximum performance for each task."

Marge held the brush, examined the bristles and agreed that these bristles were far superior to any toilet brush she had ever seen.

"And if I may, madam I'd like to give you a demonstration of all the unique advantages of this brush."

"Oh, no that's alright."

"Madam, I insist. We at Fuller Brush and I especially feel that any job that, you the housewife are tasked to do, then it is my pleasure to demonstrate how I can help to make your life easier."

"Well, okay. The bathroom is right down the hall."

The brush salesmen followed Mrs. Beazley down the hall to the bathroom.

It was after three in the afternoon when Wendy and Tommy walked home from school together. Marge felt Wendy was old enough and responsible enough to have a key to the front door to let themselves in, just in case she was out shopping or running errands.

Wendy put her key into the lock and noticed that the front door was unlocked, as soon as they were inside Wendy felt that there something wrong, the vacuum cleaner was out in the living room, in the kitchen there were all the cleaning supplies sitting on the counter, all the beds were unmade and there were piles of unwashed clothes sitting on the washing room floor. Wendy shouted out, "Mom we're home. Where are you?"

There was nothing when Tommy tried to open the bathroom door, it was locked. Something was definitely was wrong, Wendy went to the phone in the living room and called her father at the bakery, she told him that no one was home and everything was all wrong. She said that she was really scared. He told her not to worry that mom probably had to run out unexpectedly and for her to take Tommy and go next door to wait with their neighbor, Mrs. McDougall, he would be home in a couple of minutes.

Barry Beazley knew as soon as he walked thru the front door that something wasn't right, he searched the entire house and when he tried to open the bathroom door he to found it to be locked.

"Marge, it's me Barry, honey let me in."

Silence.

"Marge are you alright?"

Silence.

"All right stand away from the door, I'm breaking in."

Barry Beazley was a fireplug of a man, he stood five feet four, but weighted two hundred pounds, all of it muscle. He took three steps back, lowered his right shoulder and charged the door, when Barry made contact with the cheap unfinished wooden veneer slab door, it splintered and came off its hinges.

It took Barry several minutes to comprehend what he was looking at, there was Marge stark naked straddling the toilet facing the wall with a nylon stocking around her neck, her head tilted all the way back so she was looking up at the ceiling with a toilet brush shoved down her throat, with only the handle sticking out of her mouth.

When Roscoe and Walsh arrived, the uniforms had cordoned off the area, the ME and crime lab were already starting to process the crime scene.

The officer at the front door said, "This city is going to Hell in a handbasket. You're not going to believe this one."

"What do we have, Doc?" Roscoe asked the coroner.

"Well Detectives, it appears that Mrs. Beazley was forced into the bathroom, disrobed, made to straddle the toilet facing the wall so her back would be to the killer, then she was choked to death with a nylon stocking and as a final show of contempt had this toilet brush shoved down her throat. Of course, I'll know more after I do the autopsy."

Walsh took the brush from the coroner that had been placed in a plastic evidence bag, "It has a Fuller Brush trademark stenciled on the handle."

Taking the brush from Walsh, Roscoe looked surprised, "Fuller Brush? Ya think a Fuller Brush Man did this? That's creepy."

"Yeah, that's all we need some psycho salesman running around killing housewives in their homes."

Roscoe handed the brush back to the lab techs and said, "Well, let's go have a talk with Mr. Beazley."

One of the crime lab techs caught the two Detectives on their way out said, "Detectives, according to the husband it looks like he stole her jewelry and the money from her purse, about thirty dollars."

"Thanks, Jonesy." Walsh said.

Mr. Beazley and his children were next door at Mrs. McDougall's house, with a female officer there to give the children a softer police presence. When Roscoe and Walsh entered the home they asked the officer to take the children into the back yard while they talked to Mr. Beazley. Roscoe took off his hat and he and Walsh sat across from Barry who was sitting on the sofa.

"Mr. Beazley we are so sorry for your loss, my name is Detective Sergeant Brown and this is my partner Detective Walsh. I know this is very stressful, but it's very important that we talk while it's fresh in your memory."

"I was work, I work at the New York Bread Company over on Neptune when my daughter called and told me that there was something wrong in the house. There was the vacuum cleaner out in the living room, cleaning products sitting out in the kitchen, dirty clothes lying around, beds not made. Marge would never leave things lying about like that, plus the bathroom door was locked, thank God. I can't image what I would do if the kids would have found their mother looking like that.

"What kind of disgusting degenerate creep could do something like that? When you catch him I want five minutes alone with him, that's all just five minutes alone. I'll kill the bastard!"

Roscoe just let the man vent for a few minutes before asking the next question.

"Is there anyone that you can think of that would wish you or Mrs. Beazley any harm or that might have a grudge against either of you?"

"No, no one. Marge was the sweetest, loveliest, gentlest person you could ever meet."

"Mr. Beazley, do know if your wife was in the habit of purchasing any products from Fuller Brush?"

"Fuller Brush? Maybe, I don't really know. Why, do you think it was a Fuller Brush Man who killed my Marge?"

"Mr. Beazley at this time we don't suspect anyone, we're just gathering all the information we can and looking at all possibilities."

"Mr. Beazley is there somewhere else or someone that you could stay with for a couple days, family or friends. Think it might be best not to stay here so soon after." Walsh asked.

"My sister and her family live over in Seagate, I'm sure we can stay with her."

Roscoe handed Barry Beazley a card and said, "This is my card, feel free to call me at any time if you think of anything else. And we'll keep you posted when we have any news, but Mr. Beazley these things take time, just know that Detective Walsh and myself will be working this case and we will catch the man who did this."

"Thank you, Detectives."

After speaking with Mr. Beazley, Roscoe and Walsh canvassed the neighborhood to see if a Fuller Brush Man visited any other homes, or if anybody had seen a Fuller Brush Man in the area.

Because 2889 W. 27th Street was the last house on the corner of 27th and Mermaid it would have been easy for someone not to be seen coming off of Mermaid Avenue. The chances of one of the neighbors seeing anything that would have seen as unusual or out of place would be rare, and across the street was a grocery store with a lot of foot traffic, so anybody who saw a salesman walking up to a house wouldn't think twice about it.

Captain O'Rourke stuck his head into Roscoe's office, where he and Walsh were going over the case.

"How's it going boys?"

"Well, we think we might be dealing with a crazed Fuller Brush Man running loose in our fair city." Walsh said.

"Geeze, I hope not. I'd hate to alert people that a killer door-to-door salesman is out there, can you imagine the effect that would create, hundreds maybe thousands of door-to-door salesmen would basically be out of a job. Even after we caught him, women will be terrified to allow a salesman into their homes. I pray that you're wrong Walsh, but if you're right, we better catch this crazy mother a sap."

"We haven't gotten the lab reports or the coroner's report yet either, probably later today. Meanwhile, Walsh and I are going thru past cases and looking for people with similar MO's."

"Sounds like you've got it covered, let me know if you need anything."

"Sure thing Captain, we'll keep you up to speed."

‼️☗✝☼☙☠✵⚡‼️

Tony Webber, 28 was originally from a small town just outside of Toronto, Cayuga. He crossed over into the United States after he got mixed up in a bank heist gone wrong. Two of the gang of four were shot and killed outside of Fort Erie just on the Canadian side of the border in a high-speed chase after they fled the RBC Royal Bank with close to forty thousand Dollars, Canadian.

Tony was the getaway driver, and although he wasn't in the bank when one of his partners in crime shot and killed the bank guard, he was legally as guilty as the man who pulled the trigger.

Tony was fortunate enough to lose the police just long enough for him and the other accomplice to slip away from the police, they figured it was better to split up and go their directions. Rene Roux, Tony's accomplice grabbed the sack containing the money since he had the gun Tony wasn't about to complain. Rene then headed into the woods of Waverly Beach Park, while Tony ran off towards Fort Erie Beach.

Rene chose to go the wrong way, fifteen minutes into the chase on foot, he was wounded and captured. Tony managed to hitch a ride on an eighteen-wheeler over into Allentown, USA before the police could put out a description of him after Rene Roux sang like a canary.

The Royal Canadian Mounties sent out a warrant on Tony Webber, he was wanted for murder. Posters circulated all throughout New York State and in the northeast. He was a wanted man with a $10,000 bounty on his head.

Tony hitched all the way to New York City by catching rides at bus stops. Tony paid for the rides by having sex with the drivers, he learned that he could pretty much get anything he wanted by letting men use him sexually, a lesson he quickly learned in the Ontario Correctional Institute while serving a six-year stretch for B&E and assault.

He made his way to New York City and eventually to Coney Island, believing that the Mounties wouldn't think to look for him there. While walking along the boardwalk looking to connect with someone, anyone, he met Phil Hamilton a Fuller Brush Man who was standing in line at Cha Cha's Bar and Café to order lunch, Tony struck up a conversation and six hours later they were having sex and Tony moved into Hamilton's Brighton Beach apartment.

For six weeks Tony stayed at Phil's, he would clean the apartment, cook the meals, do the laundry and of course have sex on demand. Things were going well until one Tuesday night while watching television, not wanting to watch a rerun of the Fugitive or To Have and Have Not on Tuesday Night at the Movie, Phil decided to change the channel to watch the CBS News Hour. It proved to be a bad choice, there happened to be a story of a recent Canadian Bank robbery where a bank guard was killed, two robbers were shot to death, one was wounded and captured and the other fugitive was thought to have crossed over into the United States, a wanted felon named Tony Webber.

As luck would have it, Tony was in the kitchen standing next to the knife block when Phil came in screaming, "You're going to have to leave now or I'm calling the police. A bank robber?"

He shoved Tony up against the kitchen cabinets Yelling in his face. "How dare you, you're nothing be a common thief, you just needed somewhere to hide out. I want you out of here now!"

Tony reached behind him, grabbed a carving knife and jabbed it deep into Phil Hamilton's left temple, killing him instantly. Tony stood motionless in fear for over an hour trying to think what to do, he waited until 3 a.m. and carried Phil's body with the carving knife still sticking out of his head down two flights of stairs to the underground garage, where he put Phil in the trunk of his 1964 Ascot Blue Chevrolet Chevy II Nova 4-door sedan.

He drove out past JFK International Airport, past Jones Beach State Park out to Gilgo State Park, he turned off of Ocean Parkway onto the deserted Sore Thumb Entrance and parked before he reached the turn off that goes to the beach. Tony opened the trunk and pulled Phil's body out of the trunk, carried him over a hundred yards and buried him among a large area of beach saltbush, away from any pedestrian pathways.

He returned to the apartment just before sunrise, went upstairs and plopped into bed and slept like a baby.

!!🗝️✝️✳️☣️💀✖️⚡!!

Walsh dropped Roscoe off at home, they agreed that Walsh would pick him up around seven in the morning to get a jump on what they, internally called the Fuller Brush Killer.

When Roscoe entered the apartment he saw a receipt for 2 brushes, laundry detergent and an electrostatic caret sweeper from the Fuller Brush Company lying on the entranceway table. He hung up his fedora and shouted out, "Betty?"

She came quickly out of the kitchen, "Roscoe, is everything alright?"

He grabbed her and hugged her and said, "Yeah baby, I just missed you." And then kissed her.

"Aw, you're sweet, I love you, too."

"I see the Fuller Brush Man came."

"Yeah, he comes every couple months. I got a free toilet brush, pretty neat, huh?"

"I would feel better if you didn't have salesmen coming into the apartment while you're alone."

"Why? I've been buying from Jerry for over two years, now. What's wrong?"

"We had a murder of a young housewife today and we believe that it was either a Fuller Brush Man or somebody posing as one. That's why I'm a little wigged out."

"Well okay, I promise I won't let anyone in unless I know them. Like I said, I've known Jerry for over two years."

"Thank you babe, I can rest easier now. So, what's for dinner?"

"Dinner? Hmm, you men are all alike."

"What? Whatda I do?"

!!☗†✵⚰.☠✳⚡!!

Standing in front of the door stood a well-groomed, smiling gentleman who said, "Hi, I'm your Fuller Brush Man, and I have a free gift for you. May I step in a for a moment?"

"Of course, please come in."

Roscoe and Walsh had just finished going over the lab and autopsy reports from the Beazley murder when Roscoe got a call.

"Detective Brown, this is dispatch we have a 187 at 89 Dover Street. Officers at the scene."

"Roger that, on our way." Roscoe hung up the receiver.

"What's up?"

"We have a 187. Let's roll."

Just like the Beazley house, 89 Dover was located on a corner lot, the entrance was hidden from the street and the neighbors view. When they pulled up the area was taped off with the crime scene yellow tape, several uniformed officers standing around, directing traffic moving the rubberneckers moving along and keeping the gawkers and neighbors from trampling on the crime scene.

Officer Juddy was manning the front door, "Hey Roscoe, Walsh looks like our brush man struck again."

The inside of the house was an orchestrated circus of crime lab techs gathering fingerprints and any physical evidence, crime lab photographers popping off flashbulbs and the coroner was examining the body.

The body, Mrs. Sarah Wilson, widow, 55 years old, mother of two grown children, lived alone. From what they could piece together Mrs. Wilson was home alone having coffee and reading the New York Times when the assailant, posing as a Fuller Brush Man wormed his way in, then attacked and strangled her with a nylon stocking. He then disrobed her, placed her sitting in a brown Bennett Roll-Arm leather chair in the living room with her right leg touching the right arm of the chair and her left leg spread apart and hanging over the left arm of the chair. She was intentionally staged that way so that her pubic area was open so as to embarrass her. Her head was resting on the back of the chair so her head was looking upward with two bottlebrushes shoved up her nose with the wire handles protruding from her nostrils.

She had been robbed, her jewelry box was found on the floor, empty, all of her bedroom drawers had been gone thru, in the dining room there was an empty flatware chest for a set of sterling silver "English King" flatware valued at over nine thousand dollars, and two large "Crusader" style candlesticks with soup tureen worth approximately forty-five thousand.

Roscoe figured that the killer puts all the stolen items in the sample case and just walks out of the house undetected. He suspected that the murderer would want to pawn the stuff, but wouldn't hock it locally, so they sent out notices and descriptions of the stolen items to all the pawnshops in a hundred-mile radius.

The coroner was finishing up his preliminary exam when Roscoe asked him, "Doc I'm thinking that it's the same guy? What do you think?"

"I'd say yes. My guess is that he's either one crazy mother or he's staging these women as a big fuck you to the police and he does all this sick stuff so when he's caught he can plead insanity. You'll have my report in the morning."

The two detectives went and canvassed the neighbors, each taking a different side of the street. Walsh got lucky, one of the neighbors, a Mr. Barton Lester remembered seeing a 1964 Ascot Blue Chevrolet Chevy II Nova 4-door sedan parked around the corner on Hampton Avenue.

"What made you noticed this particular car, Mr. Lester?" Walsh asked.

"I used to have the exact same car until some drunk ran a red light and t-boned me last year. Sent me to the hospital with a broken leg."

"I'm sorry to hear that. You look like you're doing fine now."

"Yeah, I'm a tough old bird. If the Nazis couldn't kill me nothing can."

"You didn't happen to get the license plate number did you?"

"It wasn't numbers, it was letters. It was FBM."

"FBM, you sure?"

"Yep, FBM. I remember because those were my wife's initials before we got married. Francis Bethany Myers."

"Well, I want to thank you Mr. Lester for your help."

"Always happy to help our boys in blue."

Tony had a feeling that he may have slipped up with the car, so he drove around Brooklyn looking for a blue Nova so he could switch the plates. It took him five hours, but he found one, it was year newer than his, but beggars can't be choosers.

He drove over to Red Hook to Dukes Pawn and Tattoo Emporium on Van Dyke Street not far from the Louis Vatentino, Jr. Park and Pier.

Tony was just as surprised as Duke was when Duke looked up the value of the silver service that he was interested in pawning.

"Where did you get this stuff, Mr. Hamilton?"

"It was my grandmothers, she recently passed away and left it to me."

"Your grandmother, huh?"

"My mom's mom."

"Yeah, I know what a grandmother is."

"Oh yeah, well she died and left me all of this stuff and you know it's not me, I'm not married and well…"

"Look I don't need to hear your life's story, I'll give you five grand for the whole lot."

"Five grand?"

"Take a look around, I got knives and forks coming out of my ass. Take it or leave it."

"Ok, five grand."

"Okay, now I need to see some ID."

"Here's my driver's license, it's kinda messed up. I accidentally had them in my jeans when I did laundry."

Duke, the pawn shop owner knew from the start that this stuff was hot and this jamoke was a full-blown thief, but he figured one way or another he'll come out okay. If the cops didn't confiscate it as stolen goods, he'd hand it off for a tidy profit, if the cops did grab it and he helped them catch this schmuck, he'd be in for a nice CRIMESTOPPERS reward.

"Hey, this license is pretty fucked up, I'm gonna need to take a photograph of you, to cover my ass just in case your grandmother stole this stuff."

"Uh, alright."

But, what Tony didn't know was that Duke had a video camera rigged up so whenever anyone entered the store the camera would start to record and when they left it would shut off. He takes photographs of anyone he suspects to be a thief to cover his ass and to mess with their heads.

Tony didn't hock the jewelry, he was saving it because jewelry was easy to hide especially ones with precious stones. They were always good for greasing palms. Also, if caught he would hide the up his "prison wallet" or swallow some and collect them later.

!!⚫︎†☆⚡︎☠︎⚡︎!!

"The 1964 Ascot Blue Chevrolet Chevy II Nova 4-door sedan with license FBM is registered to a Philip Hamilton at 1130 Brighton 14 Street. And get this, he's a Fuller Brush Man." Walsh told Roscoe.

"FBM, Fuller Brush Man. Let's go pay Mr. Hamilton a visit."

"I talked to Fuller Brush's main office Roscoe, and they're concerned because he hasn't called in or hasn't been heard from in over a week."

"So maybe something has happened to Hamilton and somebody is using his identity as a Fuller Brush Man to commit these crimes."

"I'll give latent prints a call and see if they have come up with anything."

"After you check with them, let's go out to Hamilton's apartment."

Roscoe arranged for backup to meet them at Hamilton's apartment in Brighton Beach while Walsh went down to check to see if the killer's fingerprints were a match for anyone in the system.

Roscoe met Walsh at the car out front of the precinct, Walsh came walking up with a big grin on his face, "Our killer is named Tony Webber, he's 28, and Canadian. He's wanted for armed robbery and murder, they've been looking for him close to a month."

"Great, I've got backup waiting for us at Hamilton's."

Officer Boyle was waiting in the lobby for them with the buildings super, David Burns. The other officers were covering the exits. Burns took the two detectives and Officer Boyle on the elevator up to the fifth floor, apartment 507. Roscoe knocked, no one answered, so he rang the doorbell, nothing. He turned to the super and said, "Open it, then go."

They entered the apartment with guns drawn, it was empty, the place was very tidy and smelled of Fuller Brush scented moth blocks, a combination of mothballs and cedar, distinctly FB.

They found what looked to be a small amount of blood on the kitchen floor, so Boyle called in that they requested the CSI team out to 1130 Brighton 14 Street, apartment 507. Walsh found a nice photograph of Hamilton that they would use for a missing person poster. In the hall closet they discovered boxes of Fuller Brush products, but no sign of Webber. Hopefully, there would be his fingerprints somewhere in the apartment. One of the other officers radioed up that Hamilton's car was not in the garage. Walsh called into the station and had them put out an APB on Tony Webber on suspicion of murder and grand theft auto, not counting the Canadian Charges.

!! ☠️✝️☆⚡☠️✳️⚡!!

Tony Webber decided to try his luck one more time and then he would take the Fuller Brush gimmick down to Florida. It would be nice to not have to give blow jobs for rides with truckers, now he could take his time and see enjoy the scenery.

He was close to Greenpoint, so he'd do his Fuller Brush routine, make a score and then hop on the Williamsburg Bridge, zip thru Manhattan to the Holland Tunnel into Jersey and as New Yorkers say, "Bada Boom, Bada Bing" Miami here I come.

Driving past McGolrick Park on Monitor Street until he got to the corner of Monitor and Norman, there was a brown shingled home with easy access to the Williamsburg Bridge, around the corner was a deli with a parking lot so he could get the car off the street.

Cathy Turner had lived all alone in the same house that she grew up in, she was a New York City school teacher at PS110 Elementary School just two blocks away. She was getting ready to leave for school when the doorbell rang.

Cathy had never had a long term relationship with a man, everyone loved Cathy Turner, at 28 she was funny, had a great personality, kind and weight close to 250 pounds.

Everybody said that she has a beautiful face, if only she lost some weight. Lord knows she tried every diet in the book, Jenny Craig, Weight Watchers, South Beach, Atkins, Dukan, Pritikin, Stillman, you name it, she tried it. Nothing seemed to work, she was so lonely she used food as an emotional crutch. She had lots of girlfriends, but all of them had boyfriends or were married. Cathy Turner's only joy in life was teaching her second-grade class.

"Hi, I'm your Fuller Brush Man, and I have a gift for you. May I step in a for a moment?"

"I'm sorry, I'm just about to leave for work."

"Yes ma'am, I understand and believe me this won't take a minute, if I may I'll just leave you with my card, a brochure, and a free gift, it will only take a minute."

"Of course, please come in."

Cathy Turner's body was found that afternoon by a couple of her fellow teachers who thought that they would stop by and see if she was okay since she hadn't called in sick.

Cathy, like the two other victims, was strangled with a nylon stocking, she was naked bent over the sofa with a Wisk broom protruding from her rectum.

Unlike the other victims, Tony took a poker from the fireplace and caved her head in. He not only stole all of her jewelry and valued possessions, but he also stole her dignity, something Roscoe and Walsh were determined to have him pay dearly for.

While they were processing the crime scene, they received word that Webber had switched license plates, they now had the current plates that were on the 1964 Ascot Blue Chevrolet Chevy II Nova 4-door sedan. Walsh updated the APB and amending the warrant to read armed and dangerous after it was discovered that Phil Hamilton's 38 Special had been taken.

!!☠️†☆⚓☠️❀✦!!

Tony Webber was feeling pretty good; he scored some really fine pieces of jewelry from the fat chick. She was a hard one to position over that couch, 250 pounds, that pissed him off, so he took the fireplace poker and gave her a couple of good whacks in the head while she was still alive. After she had died to show his total disgust with the fat cow, he jammed a Wisk broom up her ass, that'll show her.

"I would like to see the faces on the cops when they find her fat ass up in the air with a broom sticking out." He said aloud laughing.

Tony was cruising along the New Jersey Turnpike coming up to the Swedesboro exit when he noticed the New Jersey State Trooper's car behind him with flashing it's blue and red lights.

"Oh shit!" Tony mumbled. He put Hamilton's 38 Special hidden under his right leg. He rolled down the window as the trooper approached with his hand on his revolver.

"License and registration."

" Was I speeding officer, I thought I was doing the speed limit." Tony said trying to act innocent.

"License and registration, please sir."

Tony reached into the glove box and pulled out the car's registration and handed it to the trooper.

"And your license, Mr. Hamilton."

Tony leaned to his right side to get his wallet of his left back pocket. "I have to tell you Officer, my license is a bit messed put, I accidentally had it in my pocket when I did the laundry."

Trooper Buckley knew right away that the driver's license had been manipulated.

"I'll be right back." Buckley said as he walked back to his squad car. He picked up the radio and called in, "Dispatch, this is car five four, over."

"Dispatch. Go five four, over."

"I'm at mile marker 86, I have a ten-sixty and request assistance, over."

"All units car five four is at mile marker 86 has a suspicious vehicle and needs assistance, over."

"Dispatch, this is car seven nine I'll handle."

"Roger that seven nine "

"Dispatch to unit five four, unit seven nine is responding, over."

"Roger that, over."

Tony knew the jig was up, he could either try and run and just postpone the enviable, go peacefully, or shoot it out and go out in a blaze of glory. While he sat there making up his mind he started to swallow the fat chicks rings, to be mined later.

As he was swallowing an antique jade ring, he noticed a second trooper car approaching, that's when Tony decided to make a run for it, he figured what the Hell, the car's got a full tank of gas and besides he thought it was such a beautiful day for a drive.

So as the two troopers were walking towards him, he gunned it. He started laughing as he looked in the rearview mirror seeing those two pigs running back to their cars.

And so the chase began, Tony had the Nova at just under a hundred miles an hour, in under twenty minutes he had crossed the Delaware state line. Officer Buckley had alerted the Delaware state highway patrol that they were in a high-speed pursuit. Aside from the two New Jersey troopers in pursuit, now they were being accompanied by three Delaware state police cars.

It took Tony an hour twenty to cross into Maryland where two Maryland state troopers joined the caravan.

Tony was having a great time driving recklessly, weaving in and out of traffic, looking in the rearview mirror and seeing the train of police cars behind them with their flashing lights.

Tony glanced down at his gas gauge and was surprised what good gas mileage he was getting, a squeak over 20mpg. Maybe he could do a commercial for Chevy Nova, a testimonial on what great mileage he got while hot-footing along at 98 miles per hour.

Unbeknownst to Tony, fun time was coming to end. Maryland state police had set up a sniper on the Raphelel Road overpass, so as Tony came screaming down the John F. Kennedy Memorial Highway the sniper would shoot out the front left tire.

Tony noticed a glint of light coming from Officer Castro's rifle scope on the overpass milliseconds before the left tire blew out, sending The 1964 Ascot Blue Chevrolet Chevy II Nova 4-door sedan out of control, causing the car to flip over six times end over end eventually landing upside down in a farmers field of unharvested tobacco.

Doctors thought it a miracle that Tony survived at all, he broke his back, left leg, right arm, sustained a concussion, lost six teeth and pooped out eighteen thousand dollars of jewelry.

When he finally opened his eyes, the first thing he saw was a man wearing a fedora eating a hot dog.

"Tony Webber you're under arrest for the murders of Marge Beazley, Sarah Wilson, and Cathy Turner. You have the right to remain silent. Anything you say can and will be used against you in a court of law. You have the right to an attorney. If you cannot afford an attorney, one will be provided for you. Do you understand these rights that I've explained to you?" Roscoe asked.

"Yeah."

"I'm Detective Sergeant Brown, NYPD, do you wish to speak to me, Mr. Webber?"

"No, go fuck yourself, pig." Tony quipped and closed his eyes.

Roscoe looked around to see that he and Webber were all alone, he reached over and closed the clamp to the morphine drip-feeding into the prisoner's arm that was handcuffed to the bed frame.

"Sweet dreams, asshole." Roscoe said as he left the room.

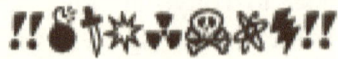

The District Attorney for the Eastern District of New York agreed to take the death penalty off the table if Tony revealed the whereabouts of Philip Hamilton's body, which he did.

The trial for the murders of Philip Hamilton, Marge Beazley, Sarah Wilson, and Cathy Turner lasted eleven weeks, it took the jury just twenty-two minutes to find Tony Webber guilty on all charges.

The judge sentenced him to four life sentences to be served separately. Tony was sent back to Canada to stand trial for the murder of the bank guard and armed robbery, he was found guilty on all charges and sentenced to eighty years to be served after he served his four life sentences in Sing Sing Correctional Facility in Ossining, New York.

After the DA made his deal with Webber not to seek the death penalty if he showed the police where Philip Hamilton's body was buried, Detective's Brown and Walsh accompanied him to Gilgo State Park to the spot where he hid the body. While they were waiting for the coroner and CSI teams to arrive Roscoe engaged Webber in small talk, then he said, "Listen Webber, this is strictly off the record, I swear to God it won't go any further than me, what was with the brushes?"

Webber thought for a moment, looked at Detective Brown, smiled and said, "I was just fucking with you. I figured if I did something really crazy, that it might throw you off, confuse you. The only one that I did for spite was the fat chick, I got pissed off because she was so hard to move. I lost it, I picked up the poker and started hitting her, then I wanted to really humiliate her, so that's why I stuck the Wisk broom in her ass."

"And you didn't sexually assault any of them, why?"

"After fourteen years in prison, I got no interest in women."

"Why Fuller Brush?"

'Why? Women will invite a total stranger into their home for a lousy ten cent plastic brush. They deserved what they got."

Roscoe was true to his word, he never told anyone, not even his partner about his conversation with Webber.

Six years into his prison sentence Tony Webber was stabbed to death by a prisoner who made a shank from a toothbrush.

Roscoe and Walsh heard about Webber's death as they were heading out to grab a couple dogs at Nathans Famous, Captain O'Rourke stopped them in the hallway and told them.

Walsh held up his hand to Roscoe and said, "Don't. Don't say it Roscoe."

"What? Say that someone gave him the brush off, you know me Jimmy, I'd never say anything as corny as that."

The Case of the HAD Matter

Joey Davis had been in and out of prison all his life; he grew up in the Bronx where he joined the children's chapter of the Seven Immortals street gang, the Young Immortals. That's where he learned the art of extortion, robbery, assault, how to handle a switchblade, the art of street fighting and all the other skills one needed to be a good gang member.

When he got out of Five Points Correctional Facility in upstate New York for assault and battery, he found that his mother had moved to Coney Island, as a condition of his parole Joey was required to live with her. Of course, it was a parole violation if he associated with the Seven Immortals.

In the late '60s, the street gangs of New York had come together to draw up a truce, they found it very advantages to stop the turf wars and just work the areas that had already been established in the turf wars of the '50s.

In the spirit of détente it was decided that when a member of one gang was forced to relocate by the police, he would be allowed to join the local gang without any animosity or retribution. So, when Joey moved in with his mother he immediately joined the Coney Island Warriors. It was like being traded from the Cleveland Indians to the New York Yankees, except becoming a Yankees you didn't have to go thru the initiation where the other members of the team beat the shit out of you.

Being a new member you had to prove your worthiness, Joey had a thin built, even though he was a skilled street-fighter his features were soft and almost effeminate, so it was decided by the Warrior's leader Geronimo that Joey would dress up like a woman, wearing a hat and dress and go out as bait, when some poor schmuck tried to hit on him, they would strike and rob the guy.

At first, Joey was reluctant to do it, but after a little persuading aka a beat down, he agreed, and he found that he was actually good at it. He started letting his hair grow long when he wasn't going out wilding as a woman he would wear it back in a ponytail. It was so successful that the other gang members stopped harassing him; they began to treat him with respect.

Joey came home one night to find his mother's man friend Tony, had given her a black eye; he was passed out lying on the couch.

"Joey, don't do nothing, he didn't mean it. He was drunk and I said something I shouldn't have. It was my fault, it's okay."

Joey went into the kitchen poured a glass of water, went into the living room and splashed the water in the man's face.

"What the…?" Tony sprang up on the couch.

"Listen to me you fat fuck, if you ever lay your hands on my mother again, I'll kill you. Do you understand? Now, get the fuck outta here!"

Tony slowly got up defiantly, he thought about making a move at the beanpole of a kid, but a split second before he was going to pounce, Joey pulled his switchblade knife out.

"Come on motherfucker, make your move. Well, come on tough guy. I know what you're thinking, this punk is just skin and bones, I can take him. Well, maybe you can and maybe you can't, are you willing to try?"

Tony just stood there, thought about it and justified not taking any action because he was still shitfaced. He reached down grabbed his jacket and left, slamming the door behind him.

!!💀🕈☼🕂🂾☠❄⚡!!

"Do we know who he is?" Roscoe asked Officer Castro as they were standing over the body.

"His driver's license says, he's Tony Montoya, he was 58 and lived at 2644 Coyle Street. We haven't got hold of any relatives yet. Looks like he's been cut up pretty bad."

"Throat cut from ear to ear, and his penis is outside of his pants." Walsh observed.

"Yeah, that was the first thing that caught my eye, too." Castro sniped.

"Has the coroner been called?" Roscoe asked.

"Yeah, right after we called it in. He should be here any moment. We looked all around and didn't find any weapon." Castro said.

Roscoe noticed that there were several footprints in the wet dirt, they looked like a man's and a women's set of prints. "Have the boys in the lab get some impressions of those footprints."

"Will do, Detective."

Walsh looked around Lenape Park, he surmised that the location where the body was discovered, the view from the neighboring houses wouldn't have been able to see much if anything at all.

"What do you think he was doing here, Roscoe?"

"Ah Lenape Park is known for 'Johns' getting a quickie, no questions asked."

Roscoe told Officer Castro that he and Walsh were going to canvas the neighborhood to see if on the off chance anybody saw anything.

Across from the park, there were dozens of semi-attached homes all facing the park, hopefully, someone saw something or maybe noticed someone unusual.

They spoke with a couple of residences that said they did see a woman in the area wearing a hat and dress. The reason they remembered her was that these days, not too many young women still wear hats, they associate hats with older women.

She was described as a young Latino or light-skinned African American, slight build, medium length dark hair, wearing a blue floral dress with a matching blue hat. They brought several of the witnesses down to the station to take a look at some mug books, but to no avail.

Roscoe and Walsh did a background check on their victim, Tony Montoya, had been arrested several times for disorderly conduct, public drunkenness, domestic violence, and a couple DUI's.

He worked as a body and fender man at Coney Island Repair and Body Shop on Neptune Avenue, they stopped by and talked to the owner, Lou Van Zandt.

"Mr. Van Zandt, I'm Detective Sergeant Brown and this is my partner Detective Walsh, we're here to talk to you about Tony Montoya."

"What did that bum do now?"

"He got himself killed." Walsh said.

"Killed? How?"

"Murdered."

"Murdered, ah that's too bad. He was a bum, but a Hell of a body and fender man, when he wasn't drunk."

"Do you know, did Mr. Montoya have any relatives?"

"No, not that I know of. I know he was living off and on with his on again, off again girlfriend, Linda Davis over on Polar Street, with her and her kid Joey, a real punk."

"Was he close with any of the other workers here?" Roscoe inquired.

"Naw, he was pretty much a loner. Once he went out drinking with some of the guys, but Tony, he was a mean drunk and nobody likes to go drinking with a mean drunk, ya know what I mean?"

"Violent?"

"Oh yeah. Got into a fight with a couple black guys over some chick. They kicked his ass pretty good. I think he got arrested on that one like I said a mean drunk."

Roscoe's handed the man a business card, "Okay thanks for your time, Mr. Van Zandt. Here's my card if you think of anything else, please call me at this number."

The two detectives drove over to 3747 Polar Street, to talk to Linda Davis and her son Joey. As they were driving up to the address, they noticed that all of the twelve attached homes front patio/driveways were all well maintained, gated, and tidy except for one, 3747.

It looked like something out of rural Mississippi, an old torn up couch, an old beat up '64 Dodge Dart sitting up on jacks, a couple tires lying around, and a German Shepherd mixed breed dog running loose. The place looked like a real dump.

When they approached the front gate they observed three men in their late twenties sitting on the couch outside wearing Warrior's jackets, the dog was snarling and barking, Roscoe held up his badge and identified himself to be a police officer.

"I'm Detective Brown of the NYPD, I'm here to see Linda Davis, is she here?"

A man with a ponytail smiled and said, "Yeah, come on in. Don't mind the dog he won't hurt you."

The other two men started laughing, one of them said, "Yeah, he's a real pussycat."

Roscoe pulled out his revolver and said, "Listen, if that dog makes a move at me, I'll shoot it and arrest the three of you for knowingly endangering the life of a police officer."

The man with the ponytail whistled and the dog ran over to him and sat down next to him.

Roscoe and Walsh entered the yard and walked up to the three men, Roscoe asked the man with the ponytail, "Are you Joey Davis?"

"Yeah, so what, I didn't do nothing."

"Walsh, you talk to the boy genius here, I'm going to talk to Mrs. Davis."

When Roscoe entered the house he wasn't surprised to find the inside was just a messy and chaotic as the outside. The furniture was all torn and broken, piles of dirty dishes, empty beer cans, food containers and clothes lying all over the counters and floor.

He found Mrs. Davis sitting at the kitchen dinette table drinking a cup of coffee.

"Mrs. Davis, I'm Detective Brown, did you know Tony Montoya?"

She put the coffee cup down, looked up at him and asked, "Why?"

"I hate to be the one to tell you, but Mr. Montoya was found dead this morning, he was murdered."

She didn't say anything, she just picked up her cup and took a sip.

"When was the last time you saw Mr. Montoya, Mrs. Davis?"

"Last night. He got into an argument with my son Joey and left."

"What time was that?"

"Around eight."

"Did Tony give you that black eye, Mrs. Davis?"

"Oh, he didn't mean to, he was drinking and I said something that I shouldn't have. It was my fault, I deserved it."

"Nobody deserves it, Mrs. Davis."

!! 🕯️✝️✳️☘️💀✴️⚡!!

On the ride back to the precinct Walsh described his conversation with the three Warrior punks, one being Joey Davis, who until a couple of months ago was a guest at the Five Points Correctional Facility for assault and battery and is now out on parole.

"Basically, all I got was a bunch of lip. He admitted that they argued and he threatened him about mistreating his mother but said that when Tony left that was the last time he saw him. Those other low lives swore that they were with him down on the boardwalk harassing the people at the Steeplechase, how's that for an alibi? So, how did you do with Mrs. Davis?"

"It's sad Jimmy, here's a woman whose husband left her when she got pregnant, her son is a convicted felon and is destined to spend his life in and out of prison and her so-called boyfriend who used her as a punching bag ends up dead. Her life is as big a mess as her environment.

"So, do you think the kids good for it?"

"I'm thinking he's a good candidate, Tony did smack his mother around, so he's number one on my hit parade list."

"What about our witnesses who say the only suspicious characters they saw was the woman wearing a hat and dress?" Roscoe asked.

"Yeah, tis a conundrum."

"Yes, it tis. You know I think we should have a squad car cruise by Lenape Park for the next couple days and see if they spot a woman wearing a hat, we could get lucky you never know."

"Let's go back to the station and see if the lab has anything on those footprints."

"Good idea."

Roscoe and Walsh walked into the crime lab and met with Officer Barr.

"Hey, Detectives got some information on those footprints that we made casts of. It looks like one set is that of Tony Montoya and the other is that of a women's shoe, size 11."

"Size 11, how does that square up with witnesses saying that the woman they saw was medium height and had a slight built?" Asked Roscoe.

"It wouldn't necessarily be inconsistent, this particular woman may just have large feet. I wouldn't read too much into it, some people have small feet for their size and others seem to have large feet for theirs."

"Can you tell us what kind of shoe it was?"

"Well, Roscoe if I had to put money on it, I would say a ladies pump with a round toe and a 3-inch stiletto heel."

"Anything else you can tell us?"

"The victim seems to have put up a good fight, he has some defensive wounds on his hands and arms. I think the Doc said that there may be some blood under his fingernails like the Vic scratched his assailant, he's sending it down to the lab. The Doc that he'd have the full autopsy report to you first thing in the morning. But it looks like he was killed with a barber straight razor."

Roscoe looked at Walsh and shrugged his shoulders and said, "Well, I'm thinking that's a wrap for the day. Say, Betty's making meatloaf for dinner, interested?"

"Don't you think you ought to check with Betty to see if it's okay?"

"Naw, she's all the time saying that we should have you over more often. Whatda think?"

"If you're sure it's okay."

"Yeah, I'm sure."

"Okay."

Walsh found a dream parking spot right in front of the building.

"Rock star parking." Roscoe quipped."

"Honey, I'm home, and look who I brought."

"Hi Betty, are you sure it's okay, I told Roscoe to call first."

Betty smiled and gave Jimmy a kiss on the cheek, "Of course it's alright, come in and make yourself right at home. Roscoe come help me in the kitchen."

As soon as they got into the kitchen, she turned and gave him "the look".

"What?"

"Why didn't you let me know that you were bringing Jimmy for dinner?"

"What, you're always saying we should have him over more, so I just thought..."

"Ah, that was your problem, you thought. Don't think."

"Yes dear."

!!✤☗✝✸❧☠✺⚡!!

Geronimo and the Warriors have had a long-standing beef with the rival gang, the Bishops going back into the '50s. It was the Coney Island version of the feud between the Hatfield's and the McCoy's, nobody could remember what the feud was about, but all they knew was they hated each other and their honor must be upheld.

It just so happened that, just like in the movie West Side Story or even Shakespeare's Romeo and Juliet, Geronimo had the hots for one of the Bishops sisters, Acindina. Not as poetic as Maria or Juliet, but that was her name, nor was Acindina as pure as Maria or Juliet, she was actually a bit of a whore. As someone once said, love is blind, but not stupid.

Geronimo had the brilliant idea that with Pablo (Acindina's brother) dead he and Acindina could be together, but he didn't want to start a full-blown gang war, Pablo's death had to see as unrelated to the Warriors.

So, he charged Joey to go undercover, as it were, and put the whack on Pablo dressed in his hat and dress. Joey would have back up with a couple of Warriors who would be dressed as squares and not wearing the Warriors colors. The problem was where to have this killing done, they needed to get Pablo into Warrior territory. The only way to do that was with the help of Acindina, who would unwittingly lure her brother to his death.

Geronimo knew that Acindina loved rollercoaster's, and the world's best rollercoaster was the Cyclone on the boardwalk in Coney Island. She had always heard about the historic wooden rollercoaster but could never ride it due to the turf war.

Geronimo promised her and her girlfriend's safe passage, no harm would befall them, knowing that Pablo would feel that he would have to accompany her just to be safe.

The plan was when Acindina and her girlfriends were riding the Cyclone, Joey dressed in his hat and dress would entice Pablo away to an area not well lit and gut him like the pig that he was. The Warriors weren't taking any chances, they were out in full force that night as a precaution in case the Bishops tried anything, and they were ready to rumble.

It was a little after nine o'clock in the evening, the weather was beautiful, warm, not too humid with a slight offshore breeze blowing in from the south when Acindina and her two girlfriends along with Pablo holding back keeping an eye on the scene arrived. Pablo was no Einstein, but he wasn't stupid enough to enter the lion's den without some of his homeboys having his back.

Following Pablo were two Bishops, also not wearing their colors trying to blend in, without much success. They stood out like a sore thumb, as did the undercover Warriors. Soon they were all gathered at the entrance of the Cyclone staring at each other, taunting and daring each other to make the first move.

In the meantime with all the commotion between the rivals, Acindina, and her friends were finally riding the Cyclone at sixty miles an hour, screaming their heads off, Joey dressed as an attracted young woman lured Pablo away into the shadows of Astroland.

Pablo was licking his chops when this attractive woman started to flirt with him. He thought that she was hot, with her long dark hair, deep dark eyes, painted red lips, and fair skin, unlike the Hispanic girls he was used to.

"Hey, girl you liking what you see?"

She smiled, took hold of his hand and said, "Let's go somewhere where we can be alone."

Her voice was deep and sexy, seductively mysterious, Pablo would have followed her anywhere.

She took him by the hand and guided him to a secluded spot near the Ferris Wheel where they were hidden within the shadows, she got very close to him within inches, she looked him in the eyes and with her left hand unzipped his jeans and took his hard penis out, Pablo thought that he was in for the time of his life, and he was.

Pablo was getting ready for what he thought was going to be the ultimate fantasy and just when he tried to say something he felt a tickling sensation on his neck, it was the blood flowing down from where Joey had slit his throat.

Joey stepped back admiring his work and in his regular voice asked, "Not exactly the orgasm you were expecting is it asshole."

Pablo, holding his neck with his right hand tried to run for help but collapsed and bleed out in less than a minute. Joey walked out into the throngs of people walking around the amusement park and blended in with the crowd, he didn't even turn around when a teenage girl happened across Pablo's dead body and screamed.

!!☀️†☆⚓☠️✳️⚡!!

The next morning the headline for the Daily News read, "Death Behind the Wheel".

Roscoe and Walsh having just finished eating their meatloaf dinner got a call from dispatch to meet the coroner at the Ferris Wheel in Astroland.

"Sorry babe, duty calls. Dinner was delish as usual. I'll be back as soon as I can."

"Thank you, Betty for having me over, even though you weren't expecting me, it was delicious." Walsh said.

"Jimmy, you know you're invited for dinner any time, with or without an invite, right Roscoe?"

"Yes dear."

Roscoe grabbed his hat off the hat rack in the foyer, gave Betty a kiss and opened the door for Walsh to lead the way.

"Thanks again for dinner."

"Any time Jimmy, now you boys be careful."

Astroland is a normally a zoo when there's no murder, but with the extra added attraction of a dead body, it was standing room only. People were standing line to ride the Ferris Wheel just to get high enough to get a glimpse of the dead as a doornail Pablo with his dick hanging out.

"I'm sensing a pattern here." Roscoe said staring down at Pablo.

"It's got to be the same person, the odds are too great to be a coincidence." Uttered Walsh.

"Officer Castro, do we know who this upstanding young man is? I'm guessing a member of a gang."

"This here is Pablo Martinez, a former member of the Bishops, Detective Brown."

"The Bishops, what the Hell is he doing here in Warrior country, Officer Castro?"

"He and his sister, Acindina and a couple of her friends were given safe passage from the Warrior leader, Geronimo as he's sweet on Pablo's sister, but I guess not all Warriors were cool with the idea, Detective Brown."

"Do we know where the sweet Acindina can be found?" Roscoe asked.

"She's at the station, Detective Brown."

"Very good, and where might we find the Warrior king Geronimo, Officer Castro?"

"Also at the station, Detective Brown."

"Excellent work, Officer Castro."

"Thank you, Detective Brown."

"No really, Tommy excellent work."

"Thanks, Roscoe."

"And just by chance are there any witnesses?"

"Not a lot, the only person that people seem to remember is…"

"Wait, let me guess, a woman wearing a hat and dress."

"Very good, sir." Castro expressing surprise.

The coroner, Doctor Chapman and his band of merry men and women appeared on to the scene.

"Hey Walsh, Roscoe, we got to stop meeting like this."

"I hear ya Doc." Roscoe quipped.

The doctor noticed the dead man's exposed penis and said, "Seriously, we got to stop meeting like this."

'We gonna head back to the station Doc, to do some interviews. I'll read your reports tomorrow."

"Okay Roscoe, see you and Walsh tomorrow. Good night."

"Night Doc. Come on Jimmy let's go interview the Beauty and the Beast."

"Yes dear."

!!☀️†☆⚓☠️✳️⚡!!

"Acindina, I'm Detective Sergeant Brown and this is Detective Walsh, we're sorry about your brother. We want you to know that just because he was a gang member doesn't mean that we aren't going to try and catch his killer. Can you tell us what happened tonight?"

"We were told that we didn't have to worry about our safety and that we could come and ride the Cyclone."

"Who did you come here with, your brother, and?"

"My two girlfriends Maria and Isabel."

"And where are they?"

"They got frightened and went home."

"Okay, at some point we'll need to talk to them, just to see if they saw anything that might be helpful. Just so you know, you are not in any trouble, we just need to gather as much information as we can to find whoever did this, okay?"

"Yes, thank you."

" Now who told you that you would be safe?"

"Geronimo."

"Geronimo, the leader of the Warriors?"

"Yes."

"Why did he say you would be safe and could come and ride the Cyclone?"

"Because he likes me, we've been seeing each other."

"Okay, Acindina and did you see him tonight?"

"Yes, we met at the Cyclone and he was with us all the time, he didn't leave us once."

"Was your brother with all of you?"

"He was until we went to ride the rollercoaster, he doesn't like them, so he said he was going to look around, and meet us back at the entrance to the Cyclone."

"How were things between him and Geronimo?"

"They didn't like each other, but it was like a truce, there wasn't any trash talking or nothing like that, they were cool."

"Did you see any other Warriors or Bishops at the Park?"

"No."

"Did you happen to see if your brother met anyone or was talking to anyone?"

"I saw him talking to a girl, she looked pretty, but we were pretty far away."

"Can you remember what she looked like, or what she was wearing?"

"Like I said we were kinda far away. She had long brown hair, she wore a blue hat and a blue dress."

"Do you think you might recognize her if you saw her again?"

"Maybe, I don't know."

"Would you be okay if we bring in a sketch artist?" Walsh asked.

"Sure."

They two detectives left her with Officer Janet Wilson, the precinct's forensic artist while went in to talk to Geronimo.

Mateo Alvarez was born in Puerto Rico and moved to Brooklyn with his family of nine when he was six. His father was a janitor at Abraham Lincoln High School on Ocean Parkway, they lived several blocks away in a one bedroom cracker box apartment above Rancho Saint Miguel, a Puerto Rican Deli & Market located right next to the El tracks on Brighton 3rd Street. The trains ran so close, you could read the headlines of newspapers the passengers were reading as they passed by.

Mateo was the baby of the family of seven children, all girls except for him. His father wanted a boy and by God, he was going to get a boy. By the time Mateo was twelve, all his sisters had gone off and had gotten married, four to men, two to God as nuns. His father worked all hours of the day and night and Mateo needed strong male role models in his life, and there were the Warriors, a street gang of more than 200 members more than willing to add to its ranks.

Mateo started out as nothing more than an errand boy, but soon grew into a dedicated soldier and worked his way to the top. Of course on his journey to the top, he spent ten years in Attica for armed robbery, but when he returned he was a made man with status and soon took the helm. Along the way, he was given the moniker Geronimo for his gung ho and can do attitude.

"Mateo, I'm Detective Sergeant Brown and this is Detective Walsh, we want to talk to you about the death of Pablo Martinez, a former member of the Bishops. And don't give me any of this I don't know the guy bullshit, we know that you supposedly gave him and his sister safe passage to come down to Warrior territory. So, be a man and tell us if you ordered the hit on Pablo."

"Hey man, that ain't how the Warriors roll, if I had a beef with Pablo, he and I would duke it out. I wouldn't have some punk-ass bitch off him, that wouldn't be cool man, ya know."

Walsh said, "Well, it's rather convenient for you that Pablo's dead and you and his sister can now hook up without any hassles from the Bishops."

"Yeah, I guess I'm just a lucky guy."

"Did you happen to see a woman wearing a blue dress and matching hat tonight ?" Roscoe inquired.

"'Naw man, that wouldn't be cool. When I'm with my lady, I ain't eyeballing other women, that wouldn't be very gentlemanly now would it?"

"Right, I forgot you're such a gentleman."

"Right on."

"Okay Mateo, get the Hell out of here. We'll be keeping an eye on you and your gentlemen's club, ya dig?"

"Groovy."

!! ☗ †✲⚛.⚰✸⚡!!

Six weeks past and three more murders had occurred, all by the woman wearing a hat and dress. The MO's were all the same, the women would lure the men, who were all rivals of the Warriors into a dark area and kill them. They were all found with their throats cut and their penises hanging outside of their pants, but no indication that sex had occurred.

They were all rival gang members, enemies of the Warriors, all except for the killing of Tony Montoya, who was tied to Joey Davis, who is a member of the Warriors. They thought that maybe the Warriors knew a woman who was handy with a blade, it could happen but that seemed unlikely.

Roscoe was looking at Joey's file and rap sheets when he just happened to lay his mug shot down next to the drawing of that police sketch artist did.

"Hey Jimmy, I was just looking at the composite of the woman that Officer Wilson drew, come take a look, isn't there a slight resemblance to Joey Davis, if he was to dress up like a woman?"

"Yeah, he's got long dark hair, he fits the general physical description, I bet he wears a size 11 woman's shoe, which is a man's size 9. All this time we've been looking for women, good work Roscoe."

"Naw, just lucky, I'm thinking we should start following Mr. Davis. We know that all the murders so far have occurred at night, so we'll pick up his trail at six and see if we get lucky."

For the next couple of days Detectives, Brown and Walsh would tail Joey from 6 p.m. to 4 a.m. when he went back to his mom's house to crash.

They were getting frustrated, they would allow him and the other Warriors to get away with petty crimes in hopes of snagging him for murder.

It was late Saturday night when Joey left his mother's house and headed over to the Warriors haunt on Stillwell Avenue. Roscoe and Walsh sat outside parked down the street, hidden by the Coney Island Boardwalk Garden watching the comings and goings of gang members when they spotted what appeared to be a woman wearing a blue hat and matching dress being escorted out of the Warriors headquarters by two members wearing their full colors.

They all got into a 1966 Pontiac Le Mans and headed north on Stillwell Avenue until they got to Scarangella Park, they pulled in and parked across the street in the Lafayette High School parking lot.

The three of them waited in the parking lot until they saw a large black man wearing a Jester's gang jacket enter the park's west entrance, the woman dressed in a blue hat and matching dress got out of the car, walked under the EL tracks and walked to the entrance gate, just inside was a small building surrounded by maple trees that housed the men's and women's bathrooms, the man in the Jester jacket was leaning against one of the Maple trees.

Roscoe and Walsh got out of their car once they saw the woman walking towards the park. The two Warriors were still sitting in the Pontiac in the high school parking lot. The two Detectives entered the park from the south entrance where the children's playground is, they weaved their way thru the trees on the east side of the park, so as not to alert the two men in the Pontiac. Once they were parallel with the woman and the man in the Jester jacket Roscoe drew his revolver and shouted, "Police, freeze!"

The woman started to run towards the parked Pontiac. Walsh took off after her, while Roscoe went to apprehend the "Jester" who was busy trying to put his penis back into his jeans, Roscoe allowed him to finish his task before handcuffing him to the bike rack next to the toilets.

With the "Jester' under control, Roscoe ran after Walsh and the woman, Walsh made a diving tackle and both he and the woman hit the ground hard knocking the breath out of Walsh, the woman got to her feet and saw Roscoe hauling ass towards them, she knelt down and put a straight razor to Walsh's neck.

"Don't take another step or the pig dies."

Roscoe stopped, he was about twenty feet away, he held up his left hand and said, "Take it easy, don't do anything stupid, Joey."

Joey had Walsh by the collar and lifted him up so he was standing behind the Detective with his right hand holding the razor under his neck.

"Drop the gun or he dies."

Roscoe noticed that the Pontiac was gone, "Your friends in the Pontiac left you high and dry, you're all alone. Drop the razor."

Joey moved the razor under Walsh's neck so that a small trickle of blood started to run down his neck staining his white shirt.

"I said to drop the gun or I'm going to cut his…"

Joey never got to finish his sentence, Roscoe drew his 38 revolver up that he was holding down at his side so quick and fired off one round that Joey had no time to react.

The bullet hit Joey's head just above his left eye, killing him instantly.

Walsh stood motionless as Joey's body fell away from him, the razor still in his hand.

"That was a Hell of a shot Roscoe."

"Yeah, not bad for somebody who failed his last qualification test."

"What!"

"Just kidding. Boy somebody's touchy."

Roscoe examined the cut on Walsh's neck, it turned out to be superficial, but just to be safe, he was treated for possible hepatitis A, B, or C and any possible staph infections at Coney Island Hospital, which all turned out to be negative.

Back at the precinct word spread of Roscoe's prowess and deadly marksmanship, he soon obtained the nickname, Roscoe "Quick Draw" Brown. And became an NYPD legend within the Department, whenever he was asked where he learned to shoot like that, he would always say, "I watch a lot of westerns on TV."

!! 💣†✴︎⚰︎💀❋⚡!!

Detective's Walsh and Brown each received the Medal of Honor, Police Combat Cross and the Medal of Valor, Detective James Walsh was promoted to the rank of Detective Sergeant, and they continued to remain partners.

After the medal ceremony, to celebrate, Roscoe treated Walsh to lunch at Nathans Famous for a couple of chilidogs and an order of crinkle cut French fries.

"Yo Vinnie, the usual times two."

"Wow, thanks Roscoe, you really know how to party." Walsh said.

"You know Jimmy, at the time I never got to say the obvious."

"Don't say it Roscoe."

"I'm gonna say it."

"Don't."

"You know Jimmy, that really was a close shave."

THE END
for now

M. Ward Leon